THESE WICKED REVELS

LIDIYA FOXGLOVE

Make sure you don't miss a release! Sign up for my mailing list.

❀ Created with Vellum

Chapter One

❦

EVALINE

On my sister's wedding day, my mother permitted her to wear white. Alexandra had never looked so beautiful, the snowy color like a beam of light in our midst.

My mother still wore gray, and so did I. I was fourteen years old, and it was my first year fully dressed as a grown woman. I still wasn't used to the long skirt, the high collar, the stiff corset, the long lace shawl that covered my hair.

As a child, I only knew my own limited world. I thought every princess, in every kingdom, must wear gray dresses and shawls and pray every morning and every night. I thought every princess must be forbidden from reading novels and going to the theater and the balls. But one by one, my sisters came of age, and something happened to them.

I was the youngest of the twelve of us.

In fact, I was the half-sister of the other eleven. Their mother had died. My mother had replaced her. They didn't

I

care for her, but they did care for me. I was four years younger than Alexandra, and sixteen years younger than Beatrice, who was the oldest—she married when I was only three. I was their darling. Growing up, there was always someone to braid my straight black hair and explain a troublesome bit of schoolwork. Always someone to exchange a private grin with when the priest droned on, and someone to laugh with when we were supposed to be sleeping.

One by one, they went away to new kingdoms, new husbands.

When Alexandra got married, I would be alone.

I grew up in a swirl of bittersweet celebrations. I carried flowers at Beatrice's wedding when I was little. I was in the procession for Tatiana's. I watched my older sisters marry handsome princes, and a few ugly ones too. There were only so many princes to go around. I admired their beautiful white gowns and the piles of flowers, wishing I had such beauty in my life more often. I waved their carriages goodbye, knowing I might never see them again, as they went away, scattered to kingdoms all over the realm.

As Alexandra said her goodbyes, she leaned close to me and said, "Eva, I must tell you a secret. Some day, you will understand. Listen closely, all right?"

I nodded.

"Never give your mask away."

I nodded like I understood. "You mean, never let my guard down?"

"Someday you will know exactly what I mean. Have a wonderful time, but don't get too caught up in it. But this is a secret. So just remember that."

"Does it have anything to do with your worn-out dancing shoes?"

"Shh." She squeezed my shoulders. "You're too young to talk about such things. Just promise me."

"I promise," I said solemnly, although my interest was already piqued. Masks? Was I going to find out the secret of the worn-out dancing shoes?

"My poor little dove." Alexandra hugged me. "I'll miss you so much."

But she would be glad to leave.

All my sisters were.

My mother was very religious. She was from the tiny kingdom of Ondalusia, which was isolated by mountains and somewhat behind the times. The women of Ondalusia always wore a lace shawl over their head and a demure dress. They didn't believe it was proper to wear bright colors, and in fact, to be on the safe side, maybe it was better just to give up colors altogether. It was hard to tell the royalty from the nuns, they said. When my father married her, she imposed her ways on his kingdom. Torina was also quite small, a fairly inconsequential kingdom—to my father's chagrin—and had changed hands more than a few times. The people were adaptable to the whims of the new queen.

It was funny to think of my mother imposing anything. She was so very quiet. She always told me to be quiet too. But silence is imposing in its own way.

I think my mother was very content in her religious devotion. I admired her, in the sense that she never wavered from her personal path. She was very small and fair and delicate. My father was certainly in love with her. Everyone said she looked like a painting, casting her huge blue eyes to the ceiling when she prayed, sometimes

3

weeping prettily. She also had a beautiful singing voice, and she used to sing me to sleep when I was a little girl.

Maybe that was where I came to my love of music. From a young age, music called to me. But it wasn't just my ears that took delight in the church organ. The music went straight to my feet.

I dreamed of dancing, even though I knew it was an indulgent sin.

My mother didn't go to the balls, and we were all strictly forbidden. If we dared to sneak down to the ballroom, just to catch a glimpse, she would lash us and make us pray for forgiveness. The only reason my father the king held balls, she said, was because the court—the decadent, corrupt court!—expected them, and Father had to keep them happy. She said that dances were something that the faeries had started, a long time ago, as a way to woo and 'indoctrinate' human girls.

But something curious happened to each of my sisters, when they reached their eighteenth birthday. Every morning, their slippers would be worn out as if they had danced the night away. Their door was locked; guards posted outside...nothing made a difference.

My mother would question them, and they denied everything. She could never find anyone who had seen them at the ball. And yet, without fail, the worn shoes kept appearing.

She started obsessing over it until my father offered rewards to any man who could figure out what happened to his daughters' shoes. First it was a horse from the royal stables, and then it was gold and then more gold.

But no one ever figured it out.

My sisters never answered my questions, although I couldn't help but notice that they seemed happier when their shoes were worn out. They glowed with an inner light, as if they had seen something marvelous.

Where were they going?

~

Sure enough, when I turned eighteen, the invitation came the very next day following my birthday. I had just put my head down on the pillow when I felt something stiff inside the pillowcase.

I reached inside and found an envelope, sealed with wax that bore a picture of a harp.

It was not a small envelope either. How had I not noticed the imprint of it even before I put my head down? How had the chambermaids not noticed when they made my bed?

It was as if the envelope had appeared out of nowhere. *Magic.*

I carefully slid my thumb beneath the seal.

Dear Princess,

Are you content, trapped within the walls of your castle? Do you ever wonder what it might be like to dance the night away to wild song, to hear drums that pound in time with the beat of your heart, to feel a man's warm embrace as he holds you close?

If you do not, then toss this letter in the fire.

If you do, then join us! These wicked revels are meant for girls such as you. Leave the letter under your pillow and wear your slippers when you come to bed tomorrow. The gate shall open at midnight.

—*The King of the Revels*

I glanced over my shoulder, masking my excitement with my most proper face. This must be it. This was my invitation and tomorrow night I would find out where my sisters had gone to wear out their shoes.

I sobered. I was the only blood daughter of my mother. She wouldn't like this at all. In fact, it might break her heart, for me to disappoint her like this. If I was a dutiful daughter, I should give her the letter and confess.

Drums that pound in time with the beat of my heart...

Even the phrase itself was like poetry. It was what I dreamed of, to lose myself in music...

With a man's warm embrace?

I had never considered that. My mother had kept me well away from young men, kept me innocent. I had never dared to think of an embrace. It was hard to even imagine anyone embracing me. When I was dressed in my stiff gray garments and shawl, I was not like a flesh and blood person anymore. I felt like a wooden figure.

I shivered. Who was this King of the Revels? How did he sneak this letter into my room? And how would I get to the ball? There were guards posted in the hall outside my door, and more guards outside watching the palace walls.

I dropped to my knees beside the bed, clasping my hands to pray for an answer, but instead of praying, I just held the letter. My breathing was heavy, straining against the corset that Mother insisted I wear to bed, to keep my figure. My nightgown was tight around my neck and wrists.

With one thrust of my small hand, I shoved the letter under my pillow.

I shut my eyes and bit my lip. *I have done something very wrong, haven't I?*

I lifted the pillow, but the invitation had vanished. I looked everywhere, to make sure it hadn't just fallen behind or gotten caught inside the pillowcase somehow. Once I knew it was gone, I got to my feet. My body swayed slightly, as if against my will.

It felt like surrender.

Chapter Two

❦

EVALINE

The next night, as I dressed for bed, I could faintly hear the musicians playing at the ball downstairs. Father was entertaining a prince and princess from Dorvania, a kingdom known for its passionate music. He had hired extra musicians just to please them. He was particularly anxious to welcome them, since they had been on the opposing side during the recent war. Now, we were at peace, and the bonds of good will were in need of strength.

The walls of the palace were thick, so I could barely make out what the song was actually like. It was torture to me, that I could never really hear the music, all the worse since my sisters left. We used to gossip and giggle on nights like this, helping each other bear the fact that we couldn't join the festivities.

I kept my slippers on. It seemed a little wrong to have shoes on beneath the covers. My feet wriggled. It was hard to sleep. *Midnight...*

I had to wait until midnight to see if anything would happen.

Downstairs, the music went on. It was very bouncy and rhythmic but it also had a frenzied, dangerous edge to it. I had seen the Dorvanian princess earlier. She was dark and beautiful. Very demure at the official dinners, so Mother was comfortable around her—but now, I imagined her feet flying to the songs. Mother would be locked in her room, far away from it all.

I wondered if it would be hard to learn how to dance. I *felt* as if I knew, deep down in my soul. But there were steps to be learned. Maybe I would make a fool of myself.

Outside, the moon rose. It was almost full.

The clock in my room ticked quietly. I kept trying to read the face in the moonlight, counting the minutes until midnight. So many long minutes...

And then, when the hour came, I heard something beneath my bed: a grinding sound, not unlike the sound of the castle gates opening. A light appeared. I looked under the bed and saw a stairwell with burning torches. The stones that made up the floor had opened up into a passageway.

"That's impossible," I whispered.

My bed started to move of its own accord, sliding sideways, revealing the passage. I looked around warily before descending. Everything had gotten very quiet. I didn't hear the music of the ball anymore. And the clock...it had stopped ticking, frozen at the midnight hour.

Am I dreaming?

It was somewhat comforting to think that it was a dream. If it was a dream, I wasn't really breaking any rules at all.

I walked down the stairs in my nightgown and slippers.

When I reached the bottom, I was standing in front of a woodland path. Behind me, the stone steps led upward into the shadows of my room.

Surely I am dreaming now...

In the distance, I heard the most beautiful music. Bells and drums and flutes and strings, a whole band playing an ethereal dance with an irresistible pounding beat. It compelled me to push forward through the forest.

The leaves of the trees had a silvery hue that caught the moonlight. Insects and frogs trilled and chirped in the shadows. I walked into the center of the grove, and a faery maiden was waiting for me. She was the most beautiful girl I had ever laid eyes on, tall and slender as a willow, clad in a long pale gown. Her hair was a brilliant red, and while my hair was always pulled straight back into a knot, hers flowed loose and thick down her back, and her eyes were slightly slanted, her expression both wise and mischievous. She was standing very still, waiting for me, with a faint smile.

"Welcome, Princess." She held out a hand.

I felt homely beside her. I was so small and bound up, with my hair and corset. My nightgown was even a little too big for me. It used to belong to my sister Elizabeth, and was passed on to me when she got married and had a fresh new trousseau. Waste not, want not, my mother said, even for princesses.

"I am to dress you for the revels," she said. "Take off your nightgown. Take off everything."

"Where?"

"Right here. I don't have a changing room, if that's what you're thinking, but I have seen it all. Think of me like one of your handmaidens. Oh, no, I remember. Your sisters told me, none of you have handmaidens to dress you in the morning."

"I do, actually," I said. "Because all my sisters are gone and there is no one left to fasten my buttons."

"Still, you are not spoiled in the least, are you? Well." She tapped my nose. "That will end tonight. In this realm, you can have everything you have ever dreamed."

"I just want to hear the music..."

"And you shall, in just a moment. But you can't bring anything with you from home except your shoes, so I will give you a beautiful dress."

I wasn't used to anyone seeing my body. I wore a shift, which I changed myself, before my handmaiden entered the room, so I was reluctant. Especially when the faery woman was so beautiful and I still felt like a girl, pale and naive and nothing special. I reminded myself that this was a dream world, anyway.

I pulled off the nightgown, and the faery woman took it from me.

"I need help with my corset," I said.

"Of course." She made a tsking sound as she unlaced it. "I remember these Ondalusian corsets. They are the most unattractive garments I have ever seen."

Some corsets exaggerated curves. Some corsets raised up the bosom. The Ondalusian corset went around my shoulders, my breasts, and down to my hips. It didn't really enhance anything, but was purely modest. It resembled nothing so much as a cage of bone, to imprison me in perfect posture. Without it, I immediately felt downright naughty, as if I could wriggle. Wriggling was not a proper motion for a woman.

She produced—with a funny twist of her hand, like a magician's trick—a dress out of nowhere. It reminded me of a dancing costume. Unlike the long gowns that women wore at home, it had a knee-length skirt that fanned out with many small fluttering panels.

"Hold out your arms."

She pulled the dress down over my head until the skirt sat at my waist.

The white fabric of the dress was so thin that it clung blatantly to the small swells of my breasts, while the dark shape of my nipples was plain to see. It had no back at all, but went around the back of my neck, plunging low in front, but even lower in back. The skirt felt like wearing some kind of flower with many small petals. It puffed out more in the back than the front, and fell longer. In the front, beneath the skirt, my legs were bare from knees to slippers. I felt like a swan.

I covered my breasts, and the faery woman pulled my hands away. She laughed, and her laugh was like bells. "Shy little girl. You're beautiful when you blush. Don't worry. The King will be so charmed. Go on. He's waiting."

"What about— Shouldn't I have some underclothes?" I had not been wearing anything under my shift, but that was because it was thick and long. This dress was another matter.

"You won't need them."

I kept walking, although the dress made me feel like I was a different person. I had never walked around with so much of me showing. I could feel pleasantly cool night air caressing my arms and legs. When the wind blew just right, it even tried to blow up my skirt, gracing my bare bottom. I planted a hand on the back of the dress to keep it from flying upward.

I passed through the grove of silver, into a grove where the trees had leaves with a golden shimmer. I could hear the music getting louder and closer. Here, another faery woman waited for me. She had golden hair that fell to her waist, and a blue dress adorned with fresh flowers.

"Good evening," she said. "Well, well. A new princess to dress. It's been a while. I thought Alexandra was the last. I was surprised when the King said we would bring the revels back to this gate."

"The revels travel around?" I asked.

"Yes, the revels go where they are needed. And you certainly need some reveling, if anyone ever did, I'd say."

"Am I dreaming?"

"You're not *exactly* dreaming."

I could tell she wasn't going to give me a real answer to any of my questions.

"What is your name, Princess?"

"Evaline. Or, just Eva."

"Princess Eva. I am here to adorn you with jewels so you will gleam like the stars."

She walked behind me, and draped a heavy gold necklace around my throat. As with the dress, the jewelry seemed to appear out of nowhere. Gold bands fit close to my neck like a collar and draping stones fell across my collar bones and down, almost between my breasts. Gold bangles followed, adorned with tiny bells, so every movement of my hands made a small jingling sound.

She slipped my feet through anklets that were just the same. And then, she let my hair down. She put a wreath of tiny golden vines in my hair and her fingers reached under my locks, up to the nape of my neck, and gently pulled down, shaking my hair out. She wove little trailing golden vines through my hair. I stood stiffly, the gold heavy on my body, but at the same time, I felt lighter than I had ever felt.

"I'll bet you have never looked so much the princess as you do now," she said. "Go on. They're waiting."

It was the same thing my first attendant had said.

I kept getting a little tickle down my spine, a small urgent voice saying, *Maybe you shouldn't do this.*

But the music tugged me onward. And the second faery was right. For the first time in my life, I felt like a princess. My gold and jewels gleamed, my skirts rustled, and even my steps and movements grew more graceful, more conscious of myself. My entire body felt transformed into something tantalizingly free. I wished I had a mirror to see myself. If I was an obedient daughter, I would turn back, but my feet carried me forward.

Past the golden grove, I reached a forest where all the trees had translucent leaves that shimmered like diamonds. I was getting impatient to reach the music, but a third faery was waiting.

She was darker than the others. Her hair was jet black and very long, well past her waist. Her eyes were an uncanny pale shade in the moonlight, although the darkness washed everything out, so I couldn't guess how they would look by daylight. She was holding a mask, with edges shaped like leaves. They were leaves, actually, I realized now, but they were very soft, carefully formed into the proper shape to fit around my face.

"Princess," she said. "I am here to give you your mask."

The way she said it would have made me nervous, even if I hadn't remembered Alexandra's words to me. They were finally starting to make sense.

"When you are here, your mask is your self," she said. "if you give away your mask, you will belong to the king."

"Oh..."

She lifted her hands to tie the mask around my face.

"But, no one can take my mask from me?" I confirmed. "I can only give it?"

"No. It absolutely must be your decision. You will be perfectly safe and come to no harm as long as you never give up your mask. That is the rule of the revels."

I nodded. "I'm just here to dance to the music."

"Then, you are ready."

I walked forward, leaving the grove where the leaves sparkled like diamonds. The path now led to the bank of a wide, lazy river. Across the river, I could see lights in the trees and sometimes the flutter of a dancing figure. A small boat was waiting for me, tied to a stubby tree near the shore. Standing inside the boat was the most gorgeous man I had ever seen.

He was all slender muscle, his body shown off by a trim jacket that fastened with gold buttons. He didn't look like any human man I had ever seen. Clearly, he was a faery. I had never seen a faery man before, and yet I would've known, even if his ears hadn't had slight points. He had a head of thick dark curls that I instantly wanted to touch, and his lovely golden eyes drank in the sight of me like I really was the most beautiful girl who had ever been born, although I knew I was no faery. I suppose, with the mask, it didn't matter as much. He bowed at the waist and then held out a hand to me.

"Princess," he said. "I've been waiting so long to see you."

"You have?"

"Oh, yes. I thought you would never grow up. I have danced with all of your sisters, but I'm hoping the best has been saved for last. Climb in. You like the music, don't you? I can see you cocking your head to hear it, even while I'm speaking to you."

"Yes," I admitted. "My mother never lets us listen to any music except in church."

He laughed. "You are in for the night of your life."

I took his hand and stepped into the boat. It swayed under my feet, but he was steady. He was very tall and sturdy, and seemed even larger up close. As long as I gripped his hand, I didn't stumble. He lowered us both down, onto two bench seats that faced each other. My knees were between his knees; there wasn't quite enough space to avoid it. I felt the warmth of his skin brushing mine, and I smelled some exotic scent—an unknown spice. He took up the oars and started to row us to the opposite shore.

A cold breeze blew across the water. The dark points of my breasts stood out against my white dress.

His eyes raked over me, and he was intensely beautiful. He took my breath away, looking at me that way, as if he already knew me and treasured me. "What is your name, Princess?"

"I'm Eva. Evaline. Princess Evaline." I was stumbling over my own tongue, between the music and the barest touch of his legs against my bare knees. I had never even been so close to a man with a chaperone, much less all alone in a small boat.

"Princess Evaline...soon we will begin, and we won't stop until your shoes are worn through."

"How long will that take?" It sounded a little like a threat, I thought.

"You won't even notice the time going by, I promise." He laughed again. "I was warned about the princesses of Torina," he said. "You are so very careful. Your sisters told me that your mother is averse to all delights."

"Well...sort of," I admitted. It didn't seem right to

complain about my mother to a stranger, but I didn't have my sisters to complain to anymore either, and I was tired of being expected to be a saint who never complained and never had any fun. "I don't see what's so bad about danc-ing. It's just plain cruel of her to make us stay in our rooms when the rest of the court gets to dance. At least...she could let us watch."

"Watch? No, it is never enough just to watch. I'm glad I get to introduce you to the pleasures of music and dance and perhaps...other things." He brought the boat to the opposite shore, and then he leaned forward toward me. I thought he was going to touch me, or even kiss me, and I went rigid. I certainly should not let him do anything like that.

Then he grabbed the rope that was behind me and jumped out, tethering the boat again.

He offered me his hand again. "Milady. Welcome to the revels."

He kept hold of my hand as he led me through an archway of vines and to a broad clearing where the ground was packed hard by all the dancing feet. My eyes hardly knew what direction to go. Several hundred of the fair folk were dancing to the music. The ladies wore all sorts of beautiful clothing, from gossamer silks that flowed to their feet to elaborate dresses adorned with flowers and ribbons. Long hair flowed free. A few high elves were there, in fine court dress, not dancing but just watching the proceedings haughtily while sipping wine. Goblins, too, looking like vagabonds in their shabby clothes and dirty bare feet, with laughing mouths full of fangs.

But most of them were faeries, and although some might favor the elves, I thought faeries were the most attractive of all people. They had wild beauty in their eyes, strong slender bodies, grace in every movement.

They could also get you into a lot of trouble. But as long as I kept my mask, I thought, I would be safe, because faeries can't lie.

Many of the women wore masks, while none of the men did. But I was pretty sure I was the only human, male or female.

"Why am I only the human?" I asked the king.

He grinned. "Because humans don't come to the revels unless we invite them. They don't know how to get here."

"Why did you invite me?"

"Because you needed us. Don't you?" He swung me over to a table with numerous bottles of drink and poured me some wine. The dance was enough of a spectacle, but the food and drink were also something to behold. Of course, if my mother didn't like us to dance, she was even more strict about us drinking alcohol. And she liked our meals to be humble as well, but here was a table spread with fruit and desserts drenched in syrup and honey, roasted meats dripping with fat, cheese tarts and bowls of olives from the southern coast. Some of the dancers stopped to nibble on the food, but one faery man was feeding olives to a girl, dangling them above her head so she had to lift up to bite them like a begging cat. All the while, his hand was beneath the edge of her dress, fondling her breast.

My eyes widened and I looked away. The king pulled me toward him with a laugh. "Too soon, eh? The cicada has just woken up from its long sleep?"

The musicians were close to the liquor, and they were what I really wished to see. I took the wine glass, but my eyes were on them. The deft hand pounding the drum, the fingers dancing the length of a flute, the man blowing on the pipes, the bow dancing on the strings of the fiddle. The fiddler stepped forward to take a solo, the other dancers pausing to give him the center of the wooden stage. They clapped; the dancers shrieked with glee as the music grew almost too fast for them to keep up with.

My feet were already tapping. Some of the other faeries were looking at me with approval. As they danced by, they cried, "Welcome, Princess! Join our dance!"

"You waste no time, do you?" the king asked.

"Can't we dance now?"

"Anything you wish. This will wait." He put my wine down again and took me into his arms.

My body responded immediately to his. He was easily a foot taller than me, his body warm and protective and so very solid. There was just a slip of fabric between my naked skin and his strong form.

So this is what it's like to dance with a man. I had been a little chilled before, but now I was instantly warm.

His eyes swept over me again.

"You are different from your sisters, aren't you?" he whispered.

"I'm my mother's only blood child. She was a step-mother to the rest of them."

"I don't mean that. I mean—you *feel* the music..." His hand slid down my bare back and rested there, in the slight hollow, as he spun me around. "I wonder if you are the one I've been waiting for..."

"Waiting for...what?"

"Close your eyes, Princess."

I did. I let him lead my body through the motions while my ears drank in the wild, merry music. It was the best thing I had ever heard in my life. I felt like I was physically drinking it, like the wine itself, feeling it slide down and burrow into my heart and gut. He moved me faster and faster, in a swirl of dizzying motion.

"Feel that?" he asked. "Feel the energy inside you loosening? It radiates from the core of your soul. Anyone who looks at you can see it, and my people are admiring you tonight. It feeds us, to see your joy."

I opened my eyes. "It's like all my dreams have come true."

"And so they have...for tonight."

"How many times will I be allowed to come here?"

"Every night, if you like."

Until I get married. Father hadn't mentioned it yet. But now that I was eighteen, I knew he would be trying desperately to marry me off quickly, to whisk me away from this enchantment that wore holes in my shoes, although I'd heard him grumbling that there were not many good prospects on the market right now.

That didn't sound promising for me.

I wasn't looking forward to marrying some foreign prince, but the only alternative was giving my mask to the king and letting him possess me. The idea gave me a forbidden thrill, but I would never act on it. I loved it here, but it was a dream. In the faery realm, time could stop, and dances could last forever. I would never give up my real world and the people I loved to live in a dream.

Chapter Three

EVALINE

When the servants presented my mother with my scuffed and torn slippers, she questioned me with tears streaming down her face.

"Eva, please—when your sisters went dancing, I was already in fear for their immortal souls, but they were not my own flesh and blood! I beg you, tell me how this happened!"

I had just had the best night of my life, and now here I was again, all laced up and covered from head to toe. My sleeves were so stiff that I couldn't even lift my arms above my head. But last night, the King of the Revels had entwined his fingers with mine and lifted my hands to the stars.

I knew that if I wanted to see him again, I would have to do the unthinkable, and lie to my mother.

All my sisters have lied before me, and they turned out all right.

"Mother," I said. "Has it ever occurred to you that maybe I'm not the one dancing? That maybe the faeries are stealing my shoes?"

She knelt on the ground in front of me, her drab gray skirt spread around her like a wilting flower. She clutched my hands. "Do you swear that, Eva?"

Her huge eyes pierced me to the core, but if I faltered, I would never hear the music again. "I swear," I said. *Forgive me.*

I had never given her cause not to believe me, but she looked at me with a moment of uncertainty. Then she slowly got to her feet. "I know you would never lie to me, Eva. But I'm still very worried. Your father is trying to find someone to marry you as soon as he can, but currently the options are not ideal. I don't want you to go to a kingdom that has a reputation for being rife with debauchery or will do nothing for our connections. I would much rather you joined the convent."

I was horrified. "The convent? But—then I would never see anything of the world."

I knew that plea fell on deaf ears. "You don't need to see the world," Mother said. "If you could only learn to be content with the world you have been given!"

What kind of world would a convent be?

I was certainly not content with the world I had been given. I needed more. Much more. Even if it was wrong.

Before long it was midnight. I was dancing to that marvelous music in the king's arms, trying to forget the dreadful fate that threatened my daily life.

On the second night, I noticed that a girl without a mask slipping off down a forest path. And then, a little after that, a man followed her, with her mask in his hand.

I realized that was where you went if you gave up your

mask, into the darkness of the forest. But what happened there?

The king caught me looking.

"You are more curious than your sisters, aren't you?" he asked. "I see your eyes roving there... What do you think happens?"

I flushed. "I would belong to you."

"What do you think that *means*?"

"I—I really don't know."

He ran his fingers along my jaw line, from one edge of the mask to the other.

"You are beautiful, Evaline," he said. "And I don't think you know it, which is the best kind of beauty. I would love to make you *my* princess. And once you gave your mask to me, you would be allowed to venture down that path. The handmaidens of the forest would prepare you for me. Your body would be forced into submission, all control surrendered, waiting and ready for my claim. Oh, you will find it a bit dreadful, I must admit."

I felt a rush of wet heat between my legs, and shifted my position nervously, hoping he couldn't tell. I shouldn't feel this way, I knew I shouldn't...

"I wouldn't keep you waiting for long, but it would be the longest wait of your life," he said. "And when I finally come...when I come to you, Evaline, it will be to give you all the pleasures you can imagine, and many more. And that would be the first day of countless days, all devoted to your desires. Pleasure is all you would ever know."

I wrapped my arms around myself, battling against a shameful rush of wanting like I had never felt. I should have shoved him away. I shouldn't listen to a man who said such corrupting things.

"I'll have to marry a human prince," I said. "I can't—" I faltered.

He arched his brows. "Your sisters must be very happy," he said.

"I think they are," I said, unsure why he was bringing them into the conversation. "They write me letters sometimes."

"Oh, well, I just thought you would be very certain," he said. "Considering you are very certain want to follow their path and marry a human prince. You seem so sure you'd be happier married to a human man you have never even met, and shut the door to the revels." He gazed down at me. "I had hoped you would be the one to stay. There is so much more I want to share with you."

"But—this isn't the life I was meant for," I said. I was trying to be polite, but I was also starting to feel just a little bit uncertain.

"Who dictates what life you are meant for?" he asked. "In the end, no one but yourself. You could have this for your own. Music and song and feasts...you could be the Queen of the Wicked Revels. Someday."

"The Queen of..." I looked around. "What would I do? Just this? Where do you live?"

"We live here," he said. "Of course, I have a very finely appointed home with all the luxuries you would need. There is an every day world here too. But it's hidden from the revels. This is meant to be an escape from mundane concerns."

"I see." I looked around at all the other dancing faeries, and a part of me felt very alone all of a sudden. I hadn't talked to anyone here except the king, although other men looked at us jealously.

"Eva. It's only the second night." He twirled me

around. "Of course you need time to think about it." He smiled at me. He had a perfect dimple in his right cheek, and if his golden eyes seemed a little predatory at times, well—he couldn't touch me. The smile seemed to bring the music into his eyes. I relaxed again. I was getting nervous because I'd never done anything like this before, never been out all night in a man's arms and gone against my parents' wishes.

"*Why* do you dance all night?" I asked him, letting my voice grow dreamy as he spun me back against him, my back to his chest, his arms looped around me.

"Because the forest is magic, and it makes us strong," he said. "Because we are here to offer an escape to girls like you, who have never known freedom in their lives. And, because it's fun. You wouldn't know much about that, would you?"

"Not until now, no."

"Evaline..." He was meeting my eyes, and I thought he might kiss me. My lips tensed together, nervous. I wondered if I'd know what to do if he tried to kiss me. "I wish..." His voice was a whisper now.

"What do you wish, your majesty?"

"I've never seen anyone like you," he said. "Your human beauty is so pure...I ache for you, Eva. I want to make you mine. I want to give you that pleasure, such as you've never dreamed of."

His voice spoke directly into my ear, like a caress. I had never heard such a voice, as if he had been born to speak to me. Maybe I wasn't going to marry him...or give him my mask...but was he ever going to kiss me already?

My hard nipples tingled, just beneath the thin fabric of my dress. I wished he would touch me. His eyes were hungry, but his hands held back.

I knew proper princesses weren't supposed to demand kisses or anything else, but I wondered if the rules even applied out here. "Kiss me," I breathed.

He made a small growl of desire and pressed himself so close to me that I felt his hard length against me. "I can't, Eva. You are dressed to entice me from head to toe and yet I am forbidden from touching you until you give me your mask."

"What? Why?"

"Do you know why we bring the revels to your castle? It's because we can sense that you need us, as your sisters did. You have been kept so strictly, you know nothing of earthly pleasures. But we are not permitted to imprint ourselves upon you in that way. We can't be your first kiss or your first release of pleasure, unless you become one of us. My touch will burn you until you give me permission."

"That's what happens when I give you my mask? I become one of you?"

He nodded gravely. "You will be marked with faery magic. And you won't be able to go home."

"Oh..."

"I understand that it's a lot to ask of you," he said. "But...every princess marries a man from some far away kingdom. Your sisters did, didn't they? And you have never seen them since? This is the only kingdom where everything will revolve around your desires and whims."

"My mother says it is a sin to indulge ones desires and whims."

"I suppose you'll have to decide if you believe her," he said. He stroked his chin, and then smiled faintly, as if he'd lighted upon an idea. "Come with me," he said.

He led me into a part of the woods. Not the dark path where I would go if I gave him my mask, but an area where the bushes were not too dense. As we got farther away from the revels, the sound of the music grew more faint, and I started to hear something else.

A woman panting, gasping.

The king took my hand and crouched. We moved closer, keeping a low profile. I stepped on a stick or two and cringed, but it didn't seem to matter.

Up ahead, one of the faery men was straddling a faery girl. I realized it was the girl who had given her mask to the man. She was spread back across the thick root of a tree, with vines caught around her hands so they were bound over her head. Her skirts were bunched around her waist and her legs were bare. His trousers were hitched down, his pelvis pumping into her.

My eyes widened. Was it all right to watch?

Suddenly the faery woman looked over at the bushes. She saw the king there.

"Carry on, my dear," he said. "I just wanted to give the Princess a glimpse."

I was somewhat shocked that he would speak to her like that in the middle of such an intimate act, that it didn't matter if we watched them. The faery man seemed to take it as a challenge. He started pushing into her faster and deeper, until she started panting out little gasps. The man pulled the straps of her filmy dress down, baring her pale breasts to the open air and twisting her nipples between his fingers.

I was hardly breathing as I watched them. I couldn't tear my eyes away, but I stayed completely still. They knew I was there, but it was still my instinct to hide.

The king took one of my own hands in his, and guided it beneath my skirt. He pressed my fingers to the bare, hot skin between my legs. I was dripping wet. He moved my fingers along my slick nether lips.

"I can't touch you yet," he whispered. "But just imagine if I could…"

The feel of my own skin in such a state alarmed me. I never touched myself like this. It was hard to believe that my prim, stiff everyday self could have been harboring anything like this, all along. This dark, wet secret was always with me. I had never known it.

As the faery girl started to cry out, the prince urged my hand to move faster. My fingers stroked swollen, forbidden places, guided by the king's hand. My skin cried out for more. I needed more. I felt the faery's pleasure echoing in my own self. I wanted to know what it felt like to lay back and let a man take control of me like that. My breath quickened as I tried to shove the thought away.

The girl started screaming, her face flushed and blissful, the faery man thrusting his cock into her over and over.

I yanked my hand away from the king. My cheeks were burning. He drew back his hand and I could see my own slickness had dripped onto his fingers.

"I have to go," I said abruptly.

I had never seen or felt anything like that before, and in the moment, it was too much. I ran to the boat and picked up the oars myself, to flee the scene. I was burning. I was angry at the king for showing me such a thing, I told myself.

But even when I was back in my own bed, and in the morning, after I was sealed up in my stiff dress, all day I kept being aware of the feelings I had felt last night. I kept reliving the moment when my fingers had stroked myself, and the faery woman's joyous abandon.

I imagined pulling up my skirts and touching that place again, exploring the secret pulse of desire within me. But I didn't dare.

I could never let anyone know. I could never let my mother see it on my face. In the real world, I had to be the perfect, silent girl I had always been.

But it felt so wrong.

And the revels felt so right. Everyone was so light and merry. Even if...sometimes...it felt a little too dark out in the forest.

Still, maybe I did deserve a life that made me happy...

By the third night, I asked the king if I could take a break from the dances to watch the musicians play.

"Of course, my lady," he said.

I walked close to the patch of grass where the musicians were assembled, and for some time I rested my feet and just watched in rapture. They smiled at me. I think they wanted to impress me, because their music grew more boisterous for a tune or two. And then they glanced at each other and nodded, and the one woman among them brought a harp forward and began to play the most haunting song. The dancers slowed their steps, the ladies' skirts twirling to match rhythms that reminded me of crisp autumn days and waves crashing on an ocean shore and storms blowing toward our castle. All of the sensations one could feel were trapped within their instruments, and they could choose any one to give me.

When the song was done, I applauded them and curtseyed. They doffed their hats to me, except the woman, who just looked at me with a slightly strange expression. She didn't smile, and her eyes were large and a little sad. But then, she looked like that all the time.

Chapter Four

WILL

"Did you hear the latest news in town?" My sister came home with bread and ale to go with the night's stew. "The king found the youngest sister's slippers with holes in them this morning."

"Why should I care about the king's brats?" I scowled, feeling the familiar pain in my leg as I stood up to grab the basket off of her hands.

"You are such a grump, Will." She shook her head at me. "I wasn't even done with my story. This time, he's not offering gold or horses to solve the mystery. He's offering Evaline's hand in marriage and—believe it or not—the kingdom. I mean—anyone who solves the mystery could be king!"

I scoffed, popping the cork from the ale and pouring us each a cup. "I'm still waiting to hear why I'd care."

"I think you should try, Will."

I almost spat out my first swig of ale. "Try to marry the *princess?* Become king someday?"

"Well, what's the harm?" She crossed her arms. "Torina is such a speck of a kingdom. Surely you could handle it. And you know a thing or two about shoes."

I rolled my eyes. I had taken over my father's old profession as the town cobbler when I came back from the war. My days with the music troupe were certainly over, but I was of an age where I needed to settle down anyway.

"You're a smart fellow. It's worth an attempt. Better than moping around here," she said.

"I'm not moping, Jeannie, I—" I scowled, hating to admit weakness. "I just can't shake the memories."

"I know..." She immediately seemed sorry. I knew she must get tired of living with me, even though she was the one who insisted on moving in to take care of me while I was recovering. She didn't have to; her husband had left a bit of money. But I knew that, despite her cheerful front, she felt his loss deeply. The war had taken its toll on so many families in town, but life went on.

"I know what this is really about," I said. "Widow Olman's been complaining about me again, hasn't she? I can't help it if that woman tries my patience. I can't fill last minute orders for her; she's not my only customer. And those shoes I made her are excellent. I don't care what she says."

Jeannie laughed. "Oh, dear, I haven't even heard about this one, although I'm sure I will.

No, I just thought—it would be the best revenge of all to win the hand of the king's daughter and to be king someday yourself. Could you imagine? I know it's unlikely. I don't even care about the money or the title. I just want to see a smile on your face again."

"I'll get there." I tried to smile now, but it was more of a grimace. "But I don't know if being king would make me smile, exactly."

"Is your leg bothering you?"

"Not too much. I was just standing on it too long. I got plenty of work done earlier."

Every day, I thanked my stars that it wasn't worse. I'd been damned lucky. A horse stepped on my leg when I was knocked down in the Battle of Crowzen. I could have lost the leg. I could have been unable to walk again. And certainly, I could have lost my life, like so many of my fellow soldiers had that day.

No, I had healed up all right, thanks to the good fortune that a healer was nearby, and Jeannie's insistence that I rest up, drink plenty of broth—she swore by it—and generally give in to her bossy nursing.

It was the memories that haunted me. The nightmares. The visions that came day and night. Michael, bleeding to death in my arms. Ulf's brains spilled out on the field. Severed limbs, the smell of blood and death, the screams and groans of dying men being run over by carts and trampled by feet. Cries for water.

Worse still, just as I had seen my friends die, I had also taken several lives. I was following my duty and fighting for my own life, but what consolation was that when I ran my sword through a young man no different from Michael or Ulf? Those men were just on the other side, that was all. They had families that would mourn them too.

I was starting to sweat just thinking about it. All that, two years of fighting, just to squabble over one goddamn territory about twenty miles square. Now the king was entertaining one of his former foes. They'd been dancing and drinking all night. And my boyhood friends, my neighbors, the friends I made during my service: we were all just game pieces to them.

Maybe it would be pretty satisfying to marry the king's youngest brat. I knew the princesses were all pious little things, but they still didn't want for anything. If she was my wife, she could stare my scars in the face. She could rub my leg when it hurt, and when I needed a release to get my mind off the memories, I could pin her under me and drive my cock into her fragile little body.

I would glare at the king on my wedding day, and maybe he would think twice before he engaged in some bloody stalemate—or before he handed off his daughter to just anybody.

To think, I used to sing ballads about war and the glory of kings. What a joke. Kings didn't care about anyone and war was nothing but a stream of horrors.

"You know, Jeannie, maybe you're right," I said, although I suspected that maybe she just wanted to get me out of the house.

On the road to the castle, in the middle of the king's woods, an old woman walked out in front of me. I instantly slowed my steps, growing wary. As far as I knew, old women didn't live in the king's woods.

"Well met, soldier," she said.

"How did you know, grandmother?" I was instantly respectful. She had no way of knowing my limp was from a war injury. A witch, I thought.

"I see it in your eyes." She hobbled toward me. She had a walking stick in one hand and a basket draped across the other arm, and wore a tattered dress and shawl, both dyed in muted forest colors. "Are you going to see about the princess and her dancing shoes?"

"I thought I'd give it a try," I said, with a shrug. I didn't want to make a fuss about it.

"I have something for you," she said, beckoning me with a stiff finger.

I came closer, on my guard. You never could be certain with old women like this, but I thought she might be sympathetic.

She pulled out the blanket inside her basket. It was actually a cloak. One side was dull black, and the other side had a slight shimmer.

"This cloak," she said. "If you wear it with the dull side out, it will turn you invisible. Wear this so you can follow the princess when she goes to the faery realm to dance at the stroke of midnight. If you wear it the other way, it will grant you the form of a faery man. You won't even feel the pain in your leg anymore, so you can dance to your heart's content without notice. But only until the dawn. That will be tricky, because the sun never shines on the revels. But nevertheless, dawn will come for you, and you will have to go."

"How am I supposed to know when the dawn comes if the sun never shines?" I was already skeptical. I didn't like magic, especially faery magic. Time followed strange rules. Men could vanish for a day and come back ten years older.

"Do you have a clock, sir?"

"I have a pocket watch." My jaw set. Even the pocket watch brought back terrible memories. Michael told me to take it when he was dying. It was an heirloom from his father and he had no son or brother who could take it.

"Then, you can mark time. You will have about six hours. Don't lose track." She handed me the cloak and her wizened hand clutched mine. "My son," she said. "My son Michael was at the Battle of Crowzen. You soothed him with a song."

I went completely cold.

That was a private moment, and there was no way she could know about it unless she was a witch, but...it was true. I used to entertain the men sometimes with songs that were rousing or bawdy. But when Michael was dying, he asked me to sing a hymn. I had never sung anything like that to another person, but I would never refuse the request of a dying man. I liked to think he died in peace because of it.

I had not sung a note since.

"Michael..." In that instant, I stopped caring who she was, how she knew about the princess and the faeries or owned a magic cloak. I knew she understood my goal. If I was the king someday, I would never engage young men in another damnably senseless war. "I won't fail you. I'll have revenge for all of them."

"Godspeed," she said.

As I arrived at the castle, another fellow was just leaving—walking like he was in pain, his head hung in shame.

He noticed me. "Hey, are you trying to win the princess? Because you'll just end up with a public whipping when you fail."

"Whipping?" Damn it, Jeannie hadn't mentioned that a public whipping was part of the bargain. I should have read the public notice myself. I definitely should have known that the king wouldn't hand over his title to just anyone. Since I'd gotten back from the war, I let Jeannie handle the world while

I stayed home. People expected to meet the old Will, and I wasn't that man anymore. Every town has a grumpy old man who yells at people for no reason, and if I was being honest, I was shaping up into that man, and I wasn't even old yet.

"Might as well turn around," the young man said. He had more money than me, I thought. Maybe a local landowner's son. His clothes were fine, silk and deeply dyed wool. "It's impossible. I was right there in the princess's room. So was the guard. I was awake one minute, and the next minute we had both slept through the whole thing. There's an enchantment there."

"Thanks for the warning."

"It's no use trying," he persisted. "You're just going to get a whipping."

"I've had worse."

He watched me keep walking, and shook his head.

I thought about that piece of information. Something had put him to sleep. Would it go into effect if I wore the enchanted cloak and no one knew I was there?

The palace guards and the herald alike all looked at me like, *Here comes another one.* But I was announced to the king, nevertheless. I'd never had a private audience with him. I followed etiquette, bowing stiffly, but I didn't let myself be intimidated by his castle, his guards, or the splendor of the throne room. I looked him straight in the eye. He was just a balding, paunchy man.

"William the Cobbler, your majesty," the herald said.

"Ah yes." The king stroked his beard, which was mostly white by now. "Here to try your luck, William? You understand that you will be whipped when—excuse me, if—you fail to discover what becomes of my daughter each night?"

"I understand."

"You must bring me proof," the king said. "Tonight, you may sleep on the floor of her room, accompanied by a guard."

"Actually, I would rather sleep down the hall, if you don't mind."

"How are you going to figure out where she's going? We always have guards in the hall. They have never seen or heard anything amiss. My daughter is locked in her room every night."

"Please, your majesty, it is my request," I said, almost speaking through my teeth.

"Very well." He waved a hand. "That's that, then."

I was permitted to share dinner with the guards, and then given a blanket and pallet on the floor in a room down the hall from the princess' room. I still had not seen a single glimpse of the princess herself.

I threw on the cloak and watched the guard lock the princess in her room. Then I returned to my pallet and pretended to sleep, checking my watch frequently. Midnight was still a couple of hours away, so I waited. I wanted the guards to relax.

Around eleven, I decided to make my move. The guard was looking pretty sleepy and bored by that time. Occasionally I kept hearing him burp, which told me he was drinking something. Few jobs were as excruciatingly dull as being a guard.

When I put on the cloak, I could still see myself, but my skin and clothes looked a little strange and washed out. That was comforting. I knew it was working. The guard didn't even glance up.

I decided not to make an attempt to steal the key. It would be better if he opened the door to check on the princess himself. I crept over to the door and rattled the handle a little.

"Hmm?" He perked up, like he was hoping something would happen. "Princess?"

No answer from her. He took out the key and unlocked the latch, then opened the door just a little. Not enough for me to get through. "Princess?"

I could tell he was about to close it, so I quickly ducked down and shoved my way through the door, tumbling across the floor. My leg was aching, but I was in her room and he hadn't seen me. He was looking at the door like it was somehow faulty. Then he looked at the sleeping princess. Finally, he shook his head and locked it shut again.

I slowly got to my feet. Now I was locked up with the princess.

I hadn't expected her to be so tiny and vulnerable look-ing. Or so...pretty. She wasn't a conventional beauty. She was very pale, and a little sickly, like she just didn't get enough fresh air or exercise. But there was something about her delicate features, her small mouth slightly open in sleep, and her breath slowly rising and falling, that stirred a deeply protective instinct like I had never felt before.

I guess it wouldn't hurt if my future bride was pleasant to my eyes, I told myself.

I was trying to be pragmatic.

It wasn't really working.

Suddenly, I wanted to bend over and master that little mouth with my own. Yank off the covers and see what she had to offer all the way down. Her untouched delicacy was the most tempting thing I'd ever seen. I'd never felt like this about anyone before. I always supposed I'd marry a nice hearty peasant girl, a little like Jeannie, but just enough *not* like Jeannie.

Well, you couldn't get much less like Jeannie than a tiny, fragile, pampered, pious princess.

But I couldn't let this feeling change what I was doing. She was still the precious daughter of the man who had ruined the lives of so many good men. Maybe I would win her heart. Maybe I wouldn't. Either way, I was going to make her mine.

Chapter Five

EVALINE

After three nights of worn-out slippers, my father issued a decree. I knew it was coming, because he'd done the same for my sisters.

What I didn't expect was that he'd offer my hand in marriage and his kingdom besides.

I already knew that my mother was planning to send me to the convent. My father had no intention of giving up his kingdom to just anyone, I was sure of that. This decree simply meant that he had given up on a solution and wanted to take his frustration out on some greedy young men.

The first one came right away. The man slept in my room with a trusted guard accompanying him. It was terribly awkward, but I didn't worry. I knew they would fall asleep before midnight, because countless men had already tried, when my sisters' shoes were wearing out.

When midnight came, the poor man was sitting there waiting and watching me.

I clenched the covers.

What if it didn't work?

And then, I saw a sparkle of golden dust stream down upon his head. He slumped back down into an immediate snore. The guard met the same fate.

"Thank you, King," I said cheekily, suppressing a laugh at the unflattering positions they had collapsed into, before my bed moved aside to reveal the stairs.

Of course, the next day, the poor man was whipped and left in shame. I didn't dare plead his case. I knew Father would say that it would all end, as soon as I told him what had happened to my slippers.

The next day brought another man, but oddly enough, he didn't ask to sleep in my room. Maybe he hoped to catch someone attempting to enter. So I never had a look at him.

That night, as I met the faery who gave me my dancing dress, I thought I heard footsteps behind me. I kept glancing back, but I didn't see anyone.

"Did you hear anything?" I asked her.

"No, but the woods do make noises. Maybe it was a bird."

In the grove of golden leaves, I heard a twig snap. I asked the faery who gave me my jewelry, and she shook her head.

"I don't see anything. I'm sure it was nothing! The gateway to the revels closes behind you."

And in the grove of diamond leaves, I heard a funny sort of rustle. By now, I had a deep sense of misgiving. "Help me look around," I begged the dark-haired faery handmaiden. We walked all around the grove and poked the bushes with sticks.

"Here!" she laughed. "It's just a weasel in the brush. I just gave him a fright."

"Weasels don't have footsteps," I said.

"No one could have followed you, I'm sure," she said.

As always, the king met me in his boat to cross the river. He settled me onto my bench. I was starting to get very accustomed to the nightly ritual. *Comfortable,* I thought, but then, that word didn't seem right.

I was used to the king. I was attracted to him. But I wasn't...comfortable.

I really just don't know him at all, I thought. *His body is growing familiar to me, but what goes on in his head?*

"Your majesty," I said. "You know, we've never talked about..." He was frowning. It made me nervous. "Our childhoods, or our dreams, or anything like that..."

"There is something strange about this boat tonight," he said.

"Yes—I did notice that. It's sort of lopsided..." But I wasn't really thinking about the boat. I was thinking about him, and the momentous decision of whether or not to give him my mask.

"What did you eat?" He laughed before giving the oars a vigorous push.

He doesn't want to answer, I thought.

Surely I couldn't give him my mask if he wouldn't answer.

As soon as I told myself that, I immediately balked. Give up the revels? Stay in my drab little kingdom forever? Join a convent?

What happens down that wooded path? What would it feel like to be dominated completely by the king?

No, I told myself. Don't think of that.

All that mattered right now was escaping to the dance. I knew one day I would have to choose, but I didn't dare think of tomorrow.

Chapter Six

WILL

I tucked the evidence in my pocket. Three leaves: one silver, one gold, and one like a sparkling sliver of diamond. They were like nothing in the earthly realm. Even a jeweler couldn't have made them, because they had the impossibly fine detail of a real leaf, and besides that, they were somewhat flexible.

When I wasn't gathering leaves, I watched the princess make her way through the forest, staying just a step behind her. As the witch promised, my leg didn't bother me even a little in this realm, while I wore the cloak.

She shed her dowdy nightgown, baring a beautiful body, before sliding on a slip of a dress. Immediately, her footsteps were lighter. Golden ornaments were placed in her hair, and around her throat, wrists, and ankles. They reminded me a little of shackles, and my cock swelled upon seeing her that way. Finally a mask was placed on her face. Too bad. Her face was my favorite thing about her.

I drew closer as she approached a small boat. A faery man was waiting for her. I tensed immediately, seeing him extend a hand to the little princess.

A human girl shouldn't be gallivanting around half-naked with faeries. The desires and motives of faeries rarely benefited humans. Didn't she know that?

Then again, if the princess had lived such a sheltered life as people said, maybe she didn't. Or maybe she didn't care.

I could see why she liked it down here. Lights and music beckoned across the river. I'd bet money that she never saw anything so enchanting. Everyone said the queen didn't even allow the princesses to attend formal dances, much less a dance out under the moonlight.

That was the thing about faeries, I supposed. They offered something so tempting that it was easy to fall under its spell. And maybe we humans shouldn't be so quick to judge; how often did I see anything this enchanting myself?

I stepped in the boat just behind the princess. I was careful, but my weight shifted the small structure. The faery man glanced up like he could see me, but then he looked at her.

No, I didn't like him. Not the way he looked at me, not the way he looked at her.

I'd met a lot of people in my life, and I knew the look of someone who was trying to find an angle they could work. A con man, that's what faeries were at heart. Always looking for a way to get something out of somebody.

Of course, who wasn't? I guess I was doing the same.

When the boat reached the shore, I could hear the music clearly. The faery musicians were so magnificent that even I forgot what I was here for, just for a minute. I missed my days in the music troupe. It was only six years ago, but it felt like an eternity.

"Do you need a drink first, my princess?" the faery man asked Princess Evaline.

She hesitated a moment. "I'd rather just dance, your majesty," she said.

Your majesty? So, he was not just any faery man, but the king of the festivities.

He took her hands with a smile and swept her into the crowd of faery revelers. There were hundreds of them, each intriguing in his or her own way, but I was having a hard time determining if they were happy, or merely frenzied. Occasionally, some of their faces betrayed a certain strange fright.

I snuck into the forest behind the musicians and turned my cloak around.

As I settled the cloak on my shoulders, a shimmering silver light swept over me, and in its place, my own humble clothing changed into the garments of a faery noble: a dark green velvet doublet, black trousers and boots. Even my hands looked cleaner. I scoffed. A spoiled princess would be pleased, I supposed, to see a man whose hands had never known hard labor. But they still had callouses from holding tools.

I walked toward the dance. The musicians glanced at me. I wondered if they would say I was an impostor.

Women looked my way as I reached the edge of the clearing, but no one seemed shocked. People seemed to come and go in and out of the forest.

Of all the women dancing, the princess held my eyes. She looked at me, but she was with her faery man, and he didn't look like he was much for sharing.

A lithe faery girl with eyes that were almost all black

behind her mask of leaves sprung toward me on her toes. "You're new here," she said.

"I thought I'd see what goes on here."

"See...and experience." She grabbed both my hands. "Handsome strangers aren't allowed to merely observe."

"And aren't you a bold lass?" I retorted, grabbing her back. In a faery sort of way, she was the type of girl I usually liked. Girls who could hold their own.

"Yes, and you'd better keep up!" Her feet were quick, her body in a state of constant motion. We marched and jigged and reeled around the clearing, and after a few, other girls wanted to dance with me too. But my eyes kept following the princess. No one enjoyed the dancing like the princess, I could tell. Every beat of the drum, every note of the flute—she felt it down to her bones. She understood music instinctively. Her feet were so light that they didn't seem to quite touch the ground. Her dark hair, laced with the strings of golden beads, danced across her back and shoulders, and her small breasts bobbed up and down. At times she looked downright giddy.

I must have been dancing for an hour already, and she had spent the entire time in the arms of the king.

I checked my watch. Two hours? That hardly even seemed possible.

"Ooh...shiny," said the faery girl who I had been dancing with, touching my pocket watch with a quick hand. She had short, wild golden hair like a dandelion.

I put the watch away and gave her a hard look. "I stole it from a human soldier."

"You keep staring at that human girl," she said. "You like messing about with humans, do you?"

"Who doesn't?" I grinned.

47

"Good luck getting ahold of her. The king thinks he can convince her to give up her mask to him."

"What happens then?"

"He gets to claim her."

I felt a pang of desire at the very idea of claiming the little princess—lanced with jealousy at the idea of the king having her instead. I hadn't even said one word to her yet. But I had a good feeling about her...and a bad feeling about him.

"He never lets her dance with anyone else?"

"Well, he would have to let her dance if she asked you. He can't deny her unless she gives him permission. But he certainly won't like it. He is the king, after all." She smiled at me, trailing a finger down my jacket. "Why bother trying to get her mask, when there are so many girls here?"

"I just want one dance," I said. *I'd never cared much for kings, anyway.*

When the next song ended, I strode over to the musicians, relishing the enchanted perfection of my own legs. It was making me feel cocky. *Cockier than usual?* I imagined Jeannie saying.

"I don't suppose you could play me a tune?" I asked them. "Your music is so fine. I'd like to sing one, if you're willing."

"Of course," said the old faery gent who played two different drums and sometimes a clacking instrument much like spoons. "What will ye have?"

Unfortunately I had no idea which songs might originate with faeries or be known in faery lands. I tried to think of one of the most compelling songs I used to sing around the fire near our camp tents. "Do you know 'At the Edge of the River'?"

"No, but tell me the rhythm and the rest will come in as we get the hang of it. They're good at that."

I nodded. It was likely that they would know a similar song, if not the exact one, because music tended to acquire changes of lyrics or slight variations but follow similar patterns across the region. "Tum, dum, dum-de-dum," I told the drummer, tapping it on my leg. He started to pound the drum.

The faeries looked my way, and so did the princess. I had never been much for attention and didn't care for all those eyes on me, but I knew this was not a moment I could falter. I had to grab the princess by her keen ears and her dancing feet, and make her wonder who I was—so much so that she would choose me over the prince.

Chapter Seven

EVALINE

Who was this singer?

I had never seen him here before. All the men here were handsome, and he was no exception, but his expression was entirely different from the others.

He looked defiant. His brown eyes were very direct and he kept looking at me. At the same time, his low, rich voice had such feeling and charm that I was struggling to dance, because it distracted me from listening to him.

The maiden comes down to the river a-flowing
She says, o river, where are you going
The river says, maiden, I go to the sea
She says, will you carry a wish there for me?

The king tugged my feet along. I forced myself to pay attention to the dance, but my attention kept returning to the newcomer. He had the most beautiful voice I had ever heard, and I wanted to shut my eyes and listen to it, and nothing else.

When he finished the tune, many of the faeries clapped for him. "I've never heard that song before," the king said, with a slight scoff.

"I like it," I said. "Who is that man?"

"I've never seen him before either."

"I want to ask him." I broke away from the king. He was displeased, but he didn't stop me. He couldn't force me to do anything against my will.

I approached the faery singer, and despite that slight sense of anger in his eyes and the wrinkle in his brow, as if something weighed upon him, I also found him surprisingly approachable. There was a kindness to him, too, I thought. I had heard that in his voice.

Suddenly I wanted nothing more than to know what it would feel like to be in his arms instead of the king's.

I curtseyed. "That was lovely," I said.

"Thank you, milady. I could see that you enjoyed it. Your dancing was a joy to watch. It'd be my pleasure to ask you for a dance myself." No one had asked me to dance except the king. I thought it was a rule that they couldn't.

I looked for the king. He was drinking wine and talking to another young man. He looked at me, and I could tell he wasn't pleased. I smiled at him faintly, as if to assure him I was doing it just to be polite.

But in fact, I was being very truthful when I said, "It is my honor for you to ask."

I was surprised, then, when he was a little clumsy

taking my hands. It seemed as if he wasn't used to dancing. But he figured it out quickly enough, and swept me along. It was immediately different from dancing with the king. Strange to say, but it felt more honest somehow. Maybe it was the fact that he didn't quite know how to do it. Maybe it was the way he looked at me. The king was all charm and refinement. This man had a roughness to him; even the way his hands felt.

"I've never seen you here before," I said.

"No. I don't usually come," he said. He paused. "In fact, I had no intention of dancing until I saw you."

"I'm nothing special," I said. The king was one thing. The attention of two men at once was embarrassing me.

"That might be true on the face of it," he said. "You're just a little thing."

I frowned. Well, I hadn't expected him to insult me. Or was he trying to flirt? The king never talked to me except in flattery and promises of what he would give me if I stayed here forever. I didn't know how to talk to a man at all.

"But the way you dance is unexpectedly charming," he continued.

"Unexpectedly? What did you expect, if you've never met me before?"

"I've heard something about your kingdom," he said.

"What have you heard?" I guessed it wouldn't be anything good.

"Your mother is as prim and proper as they come," he said. "And I've heard that you are not even allowed to attend balls in your own palace. I heard that all you do is attend church services and perhaps embroider pillows or something like that. I expected you would follow in her footsteps, with such a strict upbringing. But here I find you, dashing around like a leaf tossed on the wind."

"You sound like you don't entirely approve."

"I do approve. I'm just, as I said, surprised. Do your parents know what you get up to?"

"They're trying to figure it out...but they won't. They tried to figure it out when my sisters used to come here. The King of the Revels protects me." I hoped it was true, but in the end, the King of the Revels couldn't protect me forever—unless I gave up my mask.

"I heard your father is offering your hand in marriage to anyone who figures it out. That doesn't worry you at all?"

"No," I said.

"Really? There isn't some poor sot after you right now?"

His voice didn't match his refined appearance, I thought. He had the accent of a working class man, not a faery nobleman. Not that I knew much about faeries.

And yet, I liked the sound of it. His voice was low, a little gruff, and strangely intimate in its lack of formality. My mother always urged me to be soft-spoken, if I spoke at all, and to be very polite to everyone. Other women at court followed suit because they wanted her favor. The men did most of the talking, as men do, but they never dropped their manners either.

I never knew what anyone was thinking on the inside. Not now that my sisters were gone.

"There is," I told him. "I haven't even laid eyes on him, though. I'm sure he'll fail like all the rest, and my father will have him whipped, and it will be very miserable. I'll have to watch." Mother didn't like that Father insisted I watch, but he was resolved. Queens ought to be able to stomach such things, he said. He was hoping to provoke me into a confession, most likely.

"Human kings," the man scoffed. "They don't really care about anything but themselves."

I bristled. "What do you know about human kings?"

"I know what I hear, Princess. They send men to war, to lose life and limb, and drag themselves home with nothing to show for it. And what then? The burden and sorrow is thrown onto wives, mothers, and sisters left behind."

"I'm sure they don't *want* to send men to war."

"Don't they? You wouldn't know it."

"It's a lot more complicated than you think." I didn't like some faery man speaking about my father that way. "I'm sure my father weighs the decision."

"Hmm. I'm not sure you know any more about it than I do."

I didn't like how true that was either. I would have liked to have known more about the workings of the kingdom, seeing that I was to be the queen someday, but women weren't educated that way in Ondalusia and my mother adhered to that strictly. *Women are not the brains of the kingdom, Eva. Women are the hearts. The moral compass. It is not your place to understand war and taxes, but only to make sure your husband's heart is right with the heavens.*

"Never mind all that," I said. "I thought you liked the way I danced. I didn't know you had a critique for me."

"It's a bad habit of mine." He glanced around, taking note of how everyone else was dancing, since we had sort of drifted off to the sidelines. Following the lead of the others, he raised one of my hands up over my head and slid his other hand around my waist. We were in procession, both facing the same way, our feet springing one way and then the other.

I sensed his mood lighten with the music. It would have been impossible not to feel lighter, with such a tune and all the other faeries laughing and prancing around us. My skirt fluttered side to side with the motion of my feet and hips, while his hand kept me steady.

It was strange how, even when he wasn't speaking, and even when his appearance was not so different from the king's, he *felt* so very different. I was aware of him in a way I never was with the king.

The king was watching us. When we whirled around past him, his eyes bored into mine and I felt a wash of shame, as if I was an adulteress.

But I had never promised myself to him. Never even chosen him.

My steps faltered a little as we swept by. The faery man sensed my anxiety. "You fear him, don't you?" He sounded angry.

"Well—"

"He has no claim on you."

"But he is the King of the Revels... You don't fear him even a little?"

"No. I'm done with fearing kings." He folded his arms around me, as if he was showing the king that he had as much right to woo me as anyone there.

A delightful shiver trailed down my body. My skin grew warm as he held me close before he spun me back out to face him.

"I don't even know your name, sir," I said, a little flustered by my physical response.

"I'll give you my name when you give me your mask,"

he said. "And you will give me your mask before the night is done, Princess. Because I know what you really want."

Oh my heavens.

The shudder that went down my body when he said that. When the king said such things, a part of me wanted to draw away from him. When this man said it, it was... pure temptation.

And a part of me hoped he was right.

Chapter Eight

WILL

I could tell immediately that I'd read the princess correctly. She was attracted to me—at least, in my perfect faery form—and she didn't want to go home. She wanted to stay here, her feet caught by the music. Someone had been telling her what to do and think, how to dress and speak, for her entire life. She was comfortable being told what to do, but she wanted someone to tell her to do the things she had never been able to do before.

Still, time was slipping by so quickly. When I had a moment to check my watch between dances, I saw that the night was already half over.

She wasn't giving the king any attention any more. He had taken up with another partner, but he kept staring at us. I would have to be careful of him. I knew he must be planning something.

"What are you doing?" Princess Eva peered around my

shoulder just as I was putting my watch away. "I thought time didn't exist in the Revels."

"It doesn't," I said hastily. "But back in my own kingdom, it does."

"Where is your kingdom?"

"Over the hills."

"Hmm. That's vague. I'm half-inclined to think you are a well-dressed vagabond."

I shrugged with good humor. "You might be right. You might be wrong. With any luck I can bring you home with me eventually. My sister will like you."

"A sister? Does she live with you?"

"For now." I nodded. I didn't mention that Jeannie had lost her husband in the war. I suspected she might remarry if she'd stop worrying over me. I told her not to, but she wouldn't be stopped.

"I don't know much about faeries," she admitted. "Except that they used to steal girls away in Ondalusia. That's why my mother's people are so adverse to temptations."

"It doesn't seem to have worked, in your case."

She smiled a little, almost unconsciously, before looking solemn. "That's why I'm not sure if I should really stay here forever. I wonder sometimes if my mother is right. If I'm making a horrible mistake in giving into my temptations. All my sisters did, but then they got married to proper princes and moved away. If I give away my mask..." She touched the leaves that framed her soulful green eyes.

"Are you asking me for advice?" I asked. "Because I might be biased..."

She blinked up at me. She looked so innocent and confused. "No. I know what you want. I just don't have anyone to talk to. My sisters would tell me to be sensible, but they were never threatened with a convent."

"A convent? Who puts a princess in a convent?"

"My mother does."

"Well, I will tell you one thing, and this is the honest truth."

"I know," she said.

"You know?"

"Faeries can't lie," she said.

"Yes. Of course." I suppressed a snort. "I used to do what I was told, right up until I stared death right in the face. That makes everything very clear. Life is too short not to seize a little happiness. Of course, you have to pick your battles, and make them good ones. Do right by your fellow man and all of that. You don't want to end up on the wrong end of the hangman's noose. But a princess shouldn't have to worry about *that*. And what's the point of sacrificing yourself to a life of unhappiness?"

She tilted her head a little. "You are a very strange faery."

"How many faeries do you know?"

"Just you and the king."

"Then you don't know which one of us is really the strange faery, do you?"

She smiled a little, shaking her head. The strands of gold in her hair shimmered. "How did you almost die?" she asked.

"In battle. Fighting for the king of my realm."

"Oh." Her eyes widened. "That's why you said all those things about kings and war."

"I said all those things because I watched my friends die. Slowly and painfully, sometimes..." I didn't really mean to talk about it again. I shouldn't have told her that I had come close to death myself. It wasn't a topic conducive to wooing a girl.

But I did like how her eyes grew uncertain and searching when I spoke of it, as if she was questioning.

"My father says that war brings men glory," she said.

"And what good is glory when you're *dead?*" I snapped the word.

She recoiled. I don't think she was used to anyone raising their voice at her. "I'm sorry..."

Idiot. I was making a total mess of being a charming prince to her. I suppose that was my problem. I wasn't good at putting up a false front, pretending everything was all right and fine when it wasn't. I only knew how to be my own true self.

I knew I was supposed to pretend that war did bring glory. Jeannie even said so, when I first came back. She wanted to pretend, for the sake of her own grief. "Can't you just...try?" she asked me, when the nightmares were so fresh that I felt as if they were eating my soul alive. "Some of the townsfolk are whispering about you."

Yes, I was supposed to pretend. That it had all meant something. That I hadn't seen men suffer and die for no real reason.

Double idiot. You don't need to charm her. You already have the enchanted leaves to prove where you've been, and then she will be yours, one way or the other. You don't need her mask.

It wasn't really that I had to win her. I *wanted* to win her.

"I'm sorry," she said. "I didn't mean to bring up bad memories. I don't really know anything about anything."

"It's fine. Some wars must be fought. It's like any other kind of fight, I suppose. Some fights have a good reason behind them, and some don't."

She smiled. "Oh, that I know. I do have eleven older sisters. Plenty of fighting to be had."

We danced a few more songs, with the king watching us all the while.

"I should dance with him," she said. "But..." She hesitated. "I must admit, I like dancing with you."

"I like dancing with you, too, Princess. In fact, I wish I could send everyone else away and have you all to myself." I was starting to get impatient, knowing time was short. I had to do something to impress her, and fast. How the hell did you win a girl's heart in six hours? I'm not sure the world's greatest rake could have done it, and I was the town cobbler, for god's sake.

"Oh..." She breathed the word. "The king might not like it, but...apparently he can't do anything about it. Maybe it wouldn't hurt to take a walk."

I sensed that this was a groundbreaking request from a girl of her upbringing, for her to suggest that we go off alone together.

I've almost got her, I thought.

Chapter Nine

EVALINE

My heart was beating like a messenger's horse as the mysterious faery man and I walked away from the revels. We didn't walk down the dark path where I would go if I gave him my mask, but close to the river bank. He entwined my fingers with his. I felt so safe with him. I couldn't explain it, but even in my bedroom surrounded by my guards, I had never felt as safe as this. *Freedom brings its own kind of safety,* I thought, with some surprise. I was safe to be myself.

The night air smelled sweet. It was warm tonight. We walked under the moon, with the forest surrounding us. It was almost too dark to see. I should have been afraid of wolves, but I got the feeling that this forest was safe. After all, sometimes I saw other faeries slipping off this way.

The mask felt heavy on my face.

Alexandra told me to never give it away...

I wondered what Alexandra really knew, anyway. She had two babies now, and a husband who bored her.

I stopped walking and looked up at the moon. "I'm scared," I whispered. "I know I shouldn't tell you this, but...I really am. I don't know what to do."

"Scared of...giving up your mask?"

"Scared of making a choice. I don't want to disappoint my parents and never see them again. I don't want to be the girl who everyone whispers about, the girl who ran away with the faeries. But...I have never been so happy as I am right now."

"Only you can decide what matters," I said. "But do you think your parents give a damn about disappointing you? They're willing to hand you off to anyone who figures out where you are tonight."

"That's...true. But only because they know no one will figure it out."

"Still quite a gamble to play with your life, isn't it?"

"I guess you do know something about that. Like your war. But at the same time, it feels so irresponsible to stay here and run away from the real world."

He looked a little surprised. "You would make a good queen, I think, if given the chance."

"Really? Oh, I don't know. I don't know anything. That's the problem. I've never had a chance to experience the world and understand wars and...everything else." I took a deep breath. "I just want to breathe like this forever. I don't want to go back to corsets and petticoats and...*sleeves*."

"That would be a crime, when you have such lovely little arms." He slid his hands down my bare shoulders, to my hands. His touch was firm enough that his fingers didn't just brush me, but stroked along my muscles. It felt nice, and it stirred things inside of me.

He leaned close to me. "Maybe you need a touch of experience in 'everything else', before you decide," he said. And then his lips met mine.

My eyes opened with surprise. I didn't know he was allowed to kiss me. The king said he couldn't kiss me until I gave away my mask, that his touch would burn me until I committed myself to the revels forever. And yet, here was a warm mouth pressed to mine, tasting sweetly of desire.

I had wanted the king to kiss me, but I wanted this man to kiss me much more. *This is what it's like to fall for someone*, I thought. It was more than a pretty face or a dance. It was opening my heart to him, all while I was dreaming of something like this. The push and pull of my mind, my heart, and my yearning body... Here, in this place, he could touch me so easily. He could take me in the grass like a faery girl.

I chased my mother's scolding voice away before it could interrupt. One kiss! One kiss couldn't hurt, especially in this land of dreams.

My lips parted easily, and before I knew it, I was kissing him just as eagerly as he was kissing me. I didn't even know that I knew how to kiss. I had thought it was mainly an occupation of the lips, but it became clear immediately that the tongue was just as important. His tongue was inside my mouth. It was so naughty...and so delicious...feeling it push into me, the surprising muscular softness of it. Did my mother ever kiss my father like this? I could not imagine she did.

His hand cupped my face, then shifted to my neck. His lips pressed against mine in a slow rhythm of desire.

Goodness—it's like—it's like what men and women do

together, except with mouths. I hadn't realized you could do such things. I felt so stupid.

I suddenly felt his hand at my waist—it had been there for a while. I just noticed it then, and that my body was just hanging there stiffly. He probably thought I was terrible at this, and I was.

I had to remedy the situation.

I brought my arms up around his neck, and as he was kissing me, he inhaled deeply, a sound of satisfaction, as he drew me closer to him. His hands stroked my hair. His fingers against my scalp felt wonderful. It was already so nice to wear my hair free, and I started breathing faster.

"Poor little princess," he said. "I thought a girl like you would have everything."

"I've never had everything."

"You have plenty of food and plenty of clothes, a warm fire and a large bedroom, cooks to feed you and time to rest when you're sick, don't you?"

I nodded.

"It *is* more than most people've got."

"Yes, but...I feel so empty on the inside..."

"I see that. But I don't think you're as empty as you feel. You've been a surprise to me." He smiled, his brown eyes as warm as his hands. I had never realized how cold so much of my life had felt. "And I'd certainly like to fill you up." His hands settled on my hips, and I felt his rigid manhood pressing against my stomach. "What an effect you have on me. I'm not usually so excitable."

He plunged his tongue into my mouth again, before I could think of anything to say. I leaned against him more closely, wanting to feel his touch in other ways. My body seemed to know things that I had never learned.

One of his hands moved to my breast. His palm slid

against the pebbled skin of my nipple there and then enveloped the soft mound, as if he relished what he felt. Then his thumb stroked over my nipple, back and forth, teasing the hard nub.

My mouth pulled away from him as I was gasping for breath. I wanted to moan, but I didn't want to make a sound. I was afraid I might bite him instead. I was feeling a little panicked, like I might faint. This was so against how I had been taught to behave, and it scared me how much I liked it. How much I wanted more and more.

"You like this, don't you, little princess?"

I was ashamed to answer.

"You can't hide from me, even with your mask. And I don't think you really want to."

He easily reached under the short, light fabric of my skirt and cupped his hand to my naked cleft. Two of his fingers dipped inside my wetness, probing out my secrets.

I gasped with shame and pushed his hand away.

"I—I thought you couldn't touch me! The king said you couldn't touch me unless I gave up my mask!"

"He was obviously wrong. You don't like it?"

The faery man caught my arm as I tried to wrestle away. "But do you really *want* to run away?" he asked. "Even in the darkness, I can see the flush of your skin. I taste your hunger to know more of life. There is one thing I won't do unless you give up your mask. You're pure, and that, I will not touch. I swear, I am a gentleman, milady, but how do you if convent life is for you if you've already been living in one all of your life?" He put his fingers to my lips, fingers slick with my own juice. My mouth trembled, but I didn't fight him. He dabbed my own arousal on my tongue.

Tears sprang to my eyes. Up until now, the revels had

only been music and dancing—temptations, Mother would say, but still a sin that the entire court indulged in. This was crossing a bridge. She would never forgive me if she knew what I had done.

I couldn't make myself pull away. In fact, my eyes met his, and I said nothing to discourage him. I had never realized it before, but this was everything the revels had promised me, everything they had been leading to.

Everything I had been wanting.

His expression changed, as if something had unfolded inside of him, and he was in awe of me. I wondered if some of his confidence was a front. Did men ever feel the way I did? So scared and uncertain and small in the world?

The thought vanished on the wind as he unclasped the hooks at the back of my neck. The thin pieces of fabric that covered my breasts fell, and now all I wore was the gold necklace. He slid his hand up my back, urging me to lean backward, and his tongue teased at my nipples, one by one, before he sucked on them outright. I was so stiff with holding back my cries. I knew he would touch me between the legs again, and find me more wet than ever. I couldn't really hide what he made me feel.

He laid me down upon the grass. I looked up at the night sky, spangled with countless stars.

"I'll tell you something men don't brag about," he said.

"What is that?"

"Although I wouldn't exactly say I'm lacking in experience...well, I've never taken a woman as a man takes his wife. And I won't, unless we are pledged to each other. But there's no harm in having a bit of fun. Men do. I don't see why you shouldn't."

He pushed up my skirts so all the ruffling petals rested across my abdomen and slid his hand between my legs

67

again. He was admiring me down there, just as if he was looking at my face. I had to look away again, biting my lip.

His thumb pushed between my folds and spread my wetness around, making a slick, shameless sound. Every bit of my skin felt swollen. His wet thumb pulsed against me there in a rapid motion. I rested my hand on my stomach like I was going to pull him away, make him stop touching me in such a way, but I never quite went that far. His touch was leading me somewhere and I had to keep going. I arched my back and bit my lip even harder.

"You're so quiet," he said.

"I—I don't want to make any noise."

"A little bit of noise is welcome in a moment like this," he said. "Tells me when I'm doing something right."

"Oh—but I—I guess I don't know if any of this is right." Was it true, what he said? Should a woman be able to have a bit of fun like a man would?

He pushed his fingers inside me again, resting them there against my unbroken maidenhood. If he wanted to, he could have split me open with one thrust of his fingers. "You don't know what you want, do you, little princess? Aren't you supposed to be queen someday?"

I writhed under his invasive touch. "I am..."

"You don't think a queen ought to be decisive? How are you supposed to make good decisions for your subjects?"

"Kings make decisions. Not queens. At least—not—"

"If you were my queen, I'd like to know what you think," he said. "But only if you think something in the first place."

"I do *think*."

"Well, what do you think about this, then? You could let a man know."

"I've never been touched this way!"

"*That*, I can figure on my own." He leaned down next to me, his hand withdrawing a little, but still lightly stroking me between the legs. "I want to make you happy. Truthfully, I'm surprised at myself."

"Why?" I shuddered. The light touch was just as tantalizing.

"I didn't come here hoping you would fall in love with me. I damn sure didn't come here expecting you'd have this effect on me. But I couldn't help it. When I saw you dancing, it was like seeing a bird set free of its cage for the first time. And now—well, I feel like you've put yourself back in the cage. I want you to let go again. Let go forever. Sing for me, lass..."

His hand was still touching me, the stroking fingers going deeper, finding a sensual rhythm. He caught the core of my desire between his thumb and finger and rolled it between his calloused hand, back and forth, the pressure slowly increasing. I shut my eyes, and I finally gave voice to the feeling. I let out a small moan.

"Mmm," he replied, a low sound of approval. "There's a girl..."

"Ohhh...ohhh..." My voice sounded like I had been crying. "Ohhh, please, sir..."

"Damn. Now, that is a sound to make a man lose control of himself. Sweet princess."

My fingers toyed with the froth of my dress as I groaned louder and louder. He built the feeling up inside me, stroke by stroke, until I felt like I would have let him do anything to me he wanted. It was as joyous as it was frightening.

"Do you want me to give you your first orgasm, Princess?"

I didn't know that word, but I understood what it

meant. I was about to explode. "Yes," I panted. "Yes, *please*..."

He pressed his mouth to the center of my desire, and sucked on it. I hadn't expected that, but it struck me like lightning. I screamed my pleasure as I looked at the stars.

Chapter Ten

WILL

I had meant to seduce her. I hadn't meant to enjoy it so much. Careful plans go awry, isn't that what they say? As she cried out with unbridled pleasure, and her bud pulsed under my tongue, a few things hit me hard.

One was that this was the princess of the realm. The pristine, untouched princess, overprotected from the day she was born. No wonder she was unraveling so quickly. She was, in fact, worse than a caged bird. Even caged birds were allowed to sing.

Two, I felt like I hardly had more control than she did. I thought I was a man of the world because I'd seen war and had a few encounters with girls in the past. But what did I really know? The girls I'd dallied with before knew what they were doing, at least as much as I did. It was a quick, emotionless escape for both of us. For the princess, I knew this was shaking her entire world. I wanted to gather her up in my arms, gaze into her eyes and then claim her mouth, as I drove my cock into her. And then I wanted to tell her I would stay by her side forever, and bring her joy like this forever. Why the hell had I promised not to take her virginity tonight?

You know why. She's the princess! And you're a man of honor, aren't you? Ha!

What are you thinking? Forget the king, Jeannie would whip you when you got home if she knew what you were up to.

Third, and worst of all by far, I had deceived her. She thought she was with a beautiful faery prince. Not the limping and very human town cobbler. When I thought she was just the king's spoiled brat, I didn't care about deceiving her. Now, I was worried about how she would look at me. If she found me wholly unappealing in my real life, I wouldn't be able to touch her again.

All in all, it had turned into a complicated mess.

But for now, I still had her, looking at me with sleepy eyes full of desire, as her cries had slowed to careful breaths.

I slid my tongue up and down her pussy folds again, spinning out her pleasure as carefully as wool. Her breathing immediately grew more rapid again, with a hitch in it, the beginnings of a fresh moan. I lapped up her sweet lusty juices, my tongue teasing her entrance with swirling motions.

"Ohhh...can it happen twice?" she asked, with the pure surprise of a girl who had no idea how deep the pleasures of the body could go. "I think it's happening again..."

That fast? She really was more than ready. I stroked her clit with the tip of my tongue and saw her lifting her own hands to her breasts, slowly grazing her nipples with her thumbs. My god, she was the most beautiful thing I'd ever seen like this, pleasuring her own pale swells, moaning and whimpering. I could tell this orgasm was not as shattering and fast as the last, but was more of a slow, trembling rise and fall.

After I had brought her past the edge twice, I shifted my body so that I was laying beside her. Her face was pure bliss, her skirt still thrown up over her waist. I gently stroked her between the legs, letting her come down to earth softly.

But I was also feeling very hungry for my own release at this point. My cock was straining my trousers, and she was looking at it like she was curious.

"Do I need to do something for you now?" she asked.

She sat up a little and reached for the outline of my cock. Her fingers trailed lightly up and down my shaft through the fabric.

I couldn't take it anymore. I unbuttoned my trousers and guided her hand around the width of me. She started running her fingers along it like she was petting a cat. "Is this right?" she asked.

"Tighter," I said. "Faster."

She had a very serious expression as she obeyed. Her arms weren't very strong. But there was something utterly charming about her sudden focus, her quickened breathing as she tried to pump her hand up and down.

And frankly, it wasn't going to take much. Just looking at her and I was close to release. Watching her innocence slowly unravel, her repression fall away; it was having such an effect on me. Maybe we weren't that different in a way. Sure, I was no innocent, but I had shut myself away and tried my best to shove down my emotions. Having her draw this out of me was more of a relief than I could say.

Her hand was slowing down as she got more tired.

She shifted position, and I realized she was bringing

her mouth to the tip of my cock. She looked at me briefly as if making sure this was all right, before wrapping her little mouth around the head.

All right? This was the most alluring thing a girl had ever done to me.

She worked her lips and tongue over me with more authority than I would have guessed. Like deep down she had been waiting for such a moment herself. I'm not sure what did me in so quickly, the sensations or just the sight of her on her knees. The princess of the realm. I was almost disappointed at how quickly I started coming into her mouth. She made a squeak of surprise.

"Don't stop," I ordered her.

She didn't. Her lips and tongue stroked up and down, firm and yet soft. I reached for her hair, which hung loose, twisting it back onto her neck as some of my cum leaked out of her lips before she swallowed the rest. Gorgeous as she was, I didn't want the king to see her all messy with my seed.

She looked rather dazed, but moved as if to kiss me. I leaned closer to her and realized my leg was a little stiff.

What time is it?

Panic swept over me as I took out the pocket watch.

I only had fifteen minutes to get out of here. I struggled to my feet, my foot catching the edge of the cloak. I almost stumbled on it and tore it off of me. *Great move, there, Will.*

"I'm sorry," I told her. "I have to leave now."

"Why? Where are you going?" she cried.

"To my home. But I'll be back tomorrow."

"Oh—" She pushed her skirt down and picked up the two pieces of her bodice, her body drawing back up into itself. "I certainly hope so, sir, because...I think I've nearly made my decision."

"Yes," I assured her. "Tomorrow. I will be very eager for tomorrow." But I was already running from her. There was no time. My leg pained me a little, but could be ignored.

I hadn't gotten her mask tonight, and I supposed it didn't matter. I had evidence: the three leaves of the enchanted forest. I would win her hand back in the real world, and then I would be at the mercy of whether she chose to love the real me.

The king rushed in front of me, blocking my progress down the dark path. He was holding a goblet of wine, and his dark hair was a little disheveled. I imagined him knocking back cup after cup in a rage.

"You," he spat. "Who are you, anyway?"

"Just a faery from another realm."

"And where do you think you're going?"

"Home."

He snorted. "Why?"

"I have business."

"Mmhm. Well, sir, I see that you failed to get her mask. But what fool of a faery dares to cross the King of the Revels? You know perfectly well that I was wooing that girl. I was this close to claiming her for my own before you showed up."

"I'm not so sure about that. I also know that you can't force her to give up her mask, and that she chose me."

"If you come back here ever again, I will kill you."

I scoffed. "How honorable of you." Maybe I should've taken his threat more seriously. I didn't take anything seriously enough by half, Jeannie would say.

He plucked at the shoulder of my cloak, and I instinctively grabbed it myself, afraid he knew that it was an enchanted cloak, and he might reveal my true self if he tore it away. But instead, he kissed me on the lips.

Not a romantic kiss by any means. It was the tight, fierce kiss that says, *Next time I see you, it shall be as enemies.*

As he drew back, his mouth spread in a slow, sly grin, and he chuckled.

"The princess is mine," he said.

Getting back proved to be a chore. I didn't dare sneak into the boat, even while invisible. I swam across the river, which luckily ran slow and did not seem to be infested with any unwanted creatures. As a result, I was a sodden mess, but the stairs back into the princess' bedroom were right where I had left them, past the three enchanted groves. In the real world, that would be a given, but in the faery world, one could never be sure.

I climbed up, only to find that at the top, the princess' bed loomed over the stairs. I had to crawl out from under it, past a few motes of dust. The faint light of dawn was just beginning to peep through the windows.

I heard a gasp.

The princess was in her bed, with her covers clutched to her neck. Her eyes were round with shock.

"Who—who—" She stammered. "How—"

"How indeed?" I snapped back. "Weren't you just at the revels?"

There it was, the strange magic that made me shiver, that reordered the laws of the universe.

She had an expression of pale horror. There was no recognition in her eyes, of course. "I'm in bed," she said, her voice shaky. "Clearly, I am in bed."

I got to my feet with a little bit of difficulty. My leg was definitely causing some trouble again. I wanted to curse, remembering how easily I had danced. But I had, at least, that much propriety in the presence of the princess.

I glanced down at myself. Yes, I was no faery gentleman anymore. The green velvet had been replaced by a plain wool vest and trousers, a working man's Sunday best.

"You're the latest one to try, aren't you?" she hissed. "How did you get down there?"

"That's for me to know, isn't it?" I retorted.

She looked even more pale than before. "Get out," she said, pointing to the door. "Get out of my room."

"Is that any way to treat the man you're going to marry?" God above, I don't know what prompted me to open my mouth like that, but I didn't like being ordered around.

"Get out!"

The door flung open immediately, and two guards dashed in and grabbed me, twisting my arms behind my back. "How did you get into the princess's room?" one of them shouted in my ear.

"I found her secret realm," I said. "Just as I said I would."

"No," she said. "No, no..." It was strange to see her now, so different in this world. Her hair was pulled back severely, so she looked like hardly more than a girl, swallowed by an oversized nightgown with dowdy ruffles at the neck and wrists. "It isn't true," she said. "I've never seen him before. He was snooping around my room while I slept."

Well, this probably isn't good, I thought, before the guards shoved me out her door.

Chapter Eleven

WILL

The guards dragged me before the king with my hands tied behind my back. And they did drag me. They had no patience for my stiff leg.

Is this any way to treat a man who fought for this country? I kept my mouth shut, remembering my own advice about the hangman's noose. But I was scowling as they finally released their hold on me, the king glaring down from his throne. The queen sat beside him, which was unusual. I'd heard that she didn't usually hold court with him. She was exactly as I imagined from accounts, small and anxious, wearing a plain black dress, offering no opinions, not even a change of expression.

"Your majesties, we caught him in Princess Evaline's room," one of the guards said.

"Yes," I said, "because I know where she's been going at night."

"Tell me," the king said, looking patient. I had a feeling

that other men had concocted a number of explanations in the past.

I twisted my hands to the side, nearly yanking my shoulders out of joint, and managed to fish out the leaves from my pocket. "I have these as evidence."

One of the guards took them from me and presented them to the king.

"At midnight," I said, "A passage opens beneath the princess's bed. It leads to a faery realm. She passes through three groves. One with leaves of silver, one with leaves of gold, and one with leaves of diamonds. Then she rides a boat across the river to meet the King of the Revels and dances the night away."

The queen reached for the small holy writ she kept in her pocket, and clutched it to her breast.

The king glanced at her with faint disapproval. "My dear, don't fear for her soul yet. We have no proof," he said sternly to her. And then to me, "How do these leaves prove anything? You could have had them made."

"Tell me who makes something like that," I asked. "And how a man like me could have afforded such fine things?"

"You might have made a bargain. You might have concocted an illusion that will fade by tomorrow. And you haven't explained to me how I will stop her from disappearing again." He placed the leaves on a decorative table beside the throne. "Surely you don't expect me to believe that a cobbler deserves to marry my daughter?"

I was so furious, I must have been very red. "What sort of evidence do you want, your *majesty*? I brought you a leaf formed from diamond! You gave your word that you would give your daughter to anyone who solved the mystery."

"You have my word, but surely you understand that I

can't 'give' my daughter to you unless the proof is absolutely indisputable."

"What if she were to confess?" I asked.

The king and queen looked at each other. I wasn't sure what their eyes were saying to each other. Probably, *We can't let her marry him. Not if he brought back the faery king himself!*

But then queen said, with a sigh, "More than anything, I want to know that my daughter is telling the truth, and that her soul has not been tempted into darkness."

"Every one of my daughters has fallen under this enchantment," the king said. "And not a one would confess. She won't confess either. Bring him to the post."

"Wait—please." I gritted my teeth as the guards tried to pull me back toward the door. "I know I can make her confess if you give me one more night."

"You want one more night? Well, that will just mean two days of whipping. It is of no concern to me if you insist on wounding yourself." He waved his hand.

I imagined Evaline, shyly beginning to embrace her pleasure, her small cries as she writhed with joy last night. And then I was annoyed at myself for thinking of that. For caring about her. Only fools enter the games of kings. I should know that.

I forced myself to think of Jeannie instead. My sister was just trying to help. She would blame herself if I came back with nothing but lashings, after she'd taken such good care of me. I had to persist for her sake. She deserved something better. And I had to keep my mouth shut, as much as I wanted to curse the king's name.

The bright sunlight in the courtyard made me squint as the guards led me to one end of the long space. A wide pillar stood out in the glaring sun, with handcuffs built into it, dangling ominously, while several chairs were under a shaded walkway within view. Moving with brisk efficiency, the guards cut the bonds at my hands so they could wrestle my shirt off. Then they pushed my chest against the pillar, fitted my hands into the cuffs, and locked them tight.

I was forced to stand shirtless, sweating under the sun, with my forehead resting against the pillar and my hands yanked up in front of me, for many long moments. My arms ached. My bad leg ached. The guards said nothing, but simply waited. Some finely clad members of the court started gathering around the shaded areas. It was a particular cruelty, to be rendered helpless and stared at by people with far more wealth than I would ever know.

Finally, the king, the queen, and the little princess came out to sit in the chairs.

I met the eyes of Princess Eva dead-on. She immediately looked down. Her cheeks were pink, her expression miserable. She looked even more wretched now than she had this morning. Her hair was not just yanked back off her face, but covered by fine black lace that cast a shadow on her eyes. Although the day was hot, stiff brocade clothing covered every inch of her from neck to wrists to feet. The edges of her white linen undergarment poked out slightly. The ridges of her corset were clearly visible under her clothes. She moved stiffly as she took her seat. I think she was overheated. Her face was shining with sweat.

How could this be my dancing girl?

If I could, I would have torn my arms from my bindings and grabbed her in my arms, sweeping her away from this oppressive place forever.

"Well, Evaline, this is your chance to confess," the king

said. "This man claims to have followed you last night through forests made of silver, gold, and diamonds. If it is true, you must say so."

She looked even sicklier than before. "I—I don't know."

All the lies must be weighing on her.

But she knew the situation. If she said it was true, then she would have to marry me. And she didn't look all that impressed by the sight of me.

What princess dreamed of marrying one of the town laborers?

This was it. I had to be honest with her. She was going to break my heart, but maybe she would take pity on me and stop the whipping.

"Princess," I called. "It's me. I danced with you last night."

Her head shot up. "What? No—that's preposterous."

"It's true. I had an enchantment placed upon me so I would look like a faery. I'm sorry for deceiving you. I know that my human form isn't what you dreamed of, but...every word I spoke to you was true. If you would allow me to be the king to your queen someday, I would give you a very happy life."

The way her eyes looked when I said that gave me a glimmer of hope. They reminded me of last night. Shy— but eager. Afraid of what she might feel, but feeling it all the same.

"If that's true," she said. "Then sing for me. Sing the beautiful song you sang for me last night!"

Her parents both shot her looks of horror.

But she hadn't noticed that yet. She was looking only at me.

Normally, I would have not have liked performing

while chained shirtless to a post, but in that moment it was only the princess and me. I was starting to feel hope of my own. Maybe she would love Will the cobbler as much as she loved the faery gentleman, after all.

But what came out of my mouth?

Not my own voice. A horrid croak.

All the surrounding members of the court burst into laughter almost immediately, drowning out the sound of my song after the first few desperate words. I was trying to clear my throat, and nothing worked. My ability to sing had vanished.

"Whip him!" the king shouted. "Lash him double for toying with me!"

The princess's face crumpled, and that was the last I saw of her before the lash bit my back like a dragon's tongue, burning with pain. I clawed at the post, determined not to scream, after I had already endured such humiliation, as the whip came down, again and again. The muscles in my arms strained. Sweat poured off me, mingling with tears that leaked from my eyes. I didn't count the strikes. Time lost all meaning.

"Curse you!" I finally screamed, when I couldn't bear anymore. And still the whip bit my raw skin, as all the demure ladies of the court watched me, their faces somber under their lace shawls, and the men gawked, hands on hips and sober expressions like they had just heard that the price of grain had gone down. This was not a court to openly relish watching a punishment, not under the eyes of their queen. But I knew human nature. Human eyes cannot help but drink in darkness when it is put before them.

And then, the crack of the whip stopped.

Had it really stopped?

Guards moved to unlock the cuffs that held my hands. The pain almost seemed worse now that it was over. My arms dropped shakily to my sides. They supported me as I stumbled down from the whipping post.

I glared at the princess one last time. She had an expression of horror, but that meant nothing, really.

In the blur of pain, the shock of the lash, I had not been able to think it all through, but now I realized what the kiss of the King of the Revels had meant.

He had stolen my voice.

Chapter Twelve

EVALINE

I had been shocked to find a man in my room that morning. Under my bed. Emerging from the passage to the faery realms. All I could think was that I had been caught. It would all be over, and I would never sing and dance again, not unless my new husband was willing to stand up to court rules, and I wasn't sure any single man was capable of that.

And this man was just some ordinary fellow from town, I thought, before he was dragged away.

It was a hot day. The maid helped me into my clothing and I felt like I was trapped in an oven. It was too much to bear. *If I get out of this today, I will give up my mask tonight. I swear it. Anything is better than this.*

I received a summons to view the man's punishment as the maid was pinning my lace shawl to my hair.

So, this man had not been able to prove anything

either. Of course, Father would never let this go through. I shouldn't have worried.

I trembled with apprehension. At least he would be the last man to suffer.

I proceeded to the courtyard, and Father opened his hand, revealing gleaming leaves that were all too familiar.

I looked at the man who was now tied to the post. *He wasn't lying. He really did follow me.*

This was my first truly good look at him. The way he was looking at me reminded me so much of the faery gentleman that I thought I might faint at the idea of *that* man. The man who spoke to me so candidly and touched me in such delicious ways, surely could not emerge in the real world. If he could...

That man, I would accept as my husband. That man, I thought, was bold enough that we could work together to shape the kingdom, King and Queen together someday.

I had never realized how much I wanted it all, until that moment. I wanted music and dancing and lovemaking that left me whimpering. I wanted to bring the joys of the revels to my own court someday, or I did not want to belong to this world at all.

But my mind quickly brought itself back to the present moment. This man had familiar eyes, yes. But he was not my faery fellow. He was a human, and he looked quite different. He was about the same height, a little more tanned and muscular, because of course he would be working by day rather than dancing about by night. His hair was medium brown, cut short enough to stay out of his eyes, slight stubble traced along his jaw. His features were handsome, but not in the faery way—more coarse, more ordinary, rather than the stuff of a moonlit dream.

Still, I kept staring at him.

Those eyes.

"Princess," he said. "It's me. I danced with you last night."

Oh, heavens.

What if...what if he was my faery? What if it really was a disguise? How many times had I noted that my unnamed lover sounded more like a working man than a faery nobleman?

And then, there was his talk of war. I knew little of faery wars, so there was no way of knowing if it rang true that a faery would have recently been fighting. But my kingdom had just sent men away to a bloody conflict a couple years back.

It would explain the slow burning anger in his eyes. Why he would fight to claim this kingdom and me for his own. He would have already given up something precious for this land, without much compensation. He would have lost friends, maybe even family.

I knew immediately how he could prove himself. And I wanted to hear him sing again, if he was the man who was beginning to capture my heart.

When he opened his mouth...

I cringed back, and shut my eyes. He couldn't sing. His voice was like a croaking frog. He was a clever man, to have followed me and gotten this far, and he was trying for all he was worth, but he could not be the man I loved. I heard the court laughing, and I felt as miserable as I had ever felt, because either way, the leaves proved the truth. He had fulfilled my father's request. If I was a creature of honor, I would confess, and marry this stranger.

But if anything else, this only deepened my resolve. I knew what I wanted. Tonight, I would have him forever.

I heard the first crack of the whip, and shut my eyes.

I am so sorry, I thought, to the poor brave man. He never cried out. *I should have never have come home at all. I should have given up my mask last night. Then you wouldn't have to suffer like this.*

Tonight, I vowed.

Chapter Thirteen

WILL

One of the guards handed me my shirt and cloak. I could feel blood dripping down my back.

"Do you still want to stay for another night of this?" the king asked, clearly expecting that he had broken me.

"Yes," I said, although even speaking seemed to hurt, as if the mere vibration of a word in my chest inflamed my wounds. Trickling blood slid toward the waist of my trousers.

"My god, he's a stubborn one," the king said. "Well... show him to the infirmary."

Guards escorted me to a room down in the basement of the castle, lined with beds. To my utter shock—and something between humiliation and relief—Jeannie was down there waiting for me.

"Will!" she cried. Her hair was in disarray. She threw down a pair of scissors—it looked like she had been helping to cut wound dressings, although there was no one in the infirmary. Jeannie was always one to offer to help.

"I set out early this morning when you didn't come back last night," she said. "I started rethinking all this. I should never have gotten you involved in some crazy plan like this. And then when I got here they told me you were taking the lash!" She glanced at my back and then shut her eyes. "Shit."

The little elderly nurse widened her eyes. My sister had a blunt tongue when she was upset; we were alike in that way.

"I'll be all right, Jeannie. I've—"

"Like hell! Look at you! This is all my fault. I thought it would—well—I don't know what I was thinking."

"I do," I said. "You were dreaming of a better life. You always do, and maybe it's crazy, but it's one of your endearing qualities. And you were thinking I need to get out and take on some ambitions. You were right. Sit down. I'll tell you the whole story." I winced as I made my way to one of the beds. I forced myself to stay quiet for a time while the nurse came over with bandages and salve. She brushed off Jeannie's attempt to help.

"Oh, Will, you're really going to go back?" Jeannie whispered, once I'd told her the tale. "In this condition?"

"Now I've got to do it," I said. "The king stole my *voice*. And she was close to giving me her mask last night. Now, by the light of day, she knows damn well that I followed her to the revels, but she would rather see me be whipped than confess. If I see her tonight, one way or another, I'll win her. I think she's planning to leave this place forever. I'm this close to having it all. So, maybe it wasn't a crazy plan at all."

"I think it sounds even crazier than it did to begin

with!" She clutched her hands together. "It seems like the king is going to give you trouble. You'd better bring a weapon."

"Sure, go and grab one from my armory," I said sarcastically. My sword was provided to me by the military and taken away when I was discharged. "I don't think the king will give me a weapon, that's certain."

"Here—I have a knife." She lifted her skirt enough to pull a sheathed knife from her boot. She always kept it with her when she went out alone, just in case she ran into bandits. I always told her one girl and one knife was no match for bandits, but I guess it made her feel better.

"You know how I always hassled you about how useless one knife is? Well, a lot of good one knife will do against a king and his subjects."

"Well...it's something," she said, her face drawn with worry now. "I didn't expect this to get so dangerous." She clutched my hand. "Will—I can't lose you too."

I squeezed her fingers back. "I'll come back. I promise. And you're going to have everything you ever dreamed of, save bringing back the dead."

She nodded, but I still couldn't stand seeing fear in her steely gray eyes. If I died, even Jeannie's tough heart would break. It wasn't an option.

Chapter Fourteen

EVALINE

I barely ate a bite at dinner. Mother blamed the whipping for stealing my appetite, and told Father I shouldn't have to watch. But the real reason, of course, was that I knew this was my last night here. Tonight, I would give up my mask and walk down that dark path. I would belong to the faery man with the beautiful voice.

Your body would be forced into submission, all control surrendered, waiting and ready for my claim...

What was going to happen to me? Would it be the same fate if I gave my mask to the singer instead of the king?

I was as excited as I was scared. Every time I thought of it, I throbbed between my legs. The revels had unleashed something in me that I didn't think could ever be ignored. I had to go there, whether I liked it or not. With all my being, I yearned to be touched again like I had last night.

When night came, I had never been so relieved. I slipped down the stairs as I always did, and met the faery handmaidens, as I always did. But it felt so different, because this time, I knew I would not be coming back.

I wondered if that human man was following me again. It must have been him I was hearing in the grove behind me, his weight that had bogged down the boat. He must possess some sort of invisibility enchantment. I tried to get into the boat quickly, and told the king, "Hurry."

But he was in no hurry. He was looking at me, plainly displeased. "In a hurry to see someone?"

"I'm sorry, your majesty, I just..."

"I don't know who that man was." He paused. "Are you planning on giving him your mask?"

"I don't mean to offend you. I have so enjoyed dancing with you. I just thought...his music was very beautiful."

"You belong to me."

"No, I don't! I don't have to keep coming. None of my sisters stayed here, as you well know."

I felt the weight of the boat shifting behind me, as if someone was climbing in. The king suddenly shoved my head down and swept his oar just over me. I felt the boat rock wildly, as if someone was dodging the oar. I shrieked as the king swung the oar again, and the boat tipped in the struggle. Behind me, a body splashed into the water, and a second later, I lost my balance myself. The boat flipped over and we were all in the water. My skirt was billowing up, leaving my lower half quite naked. I tried to shove it down.

I looked around and saw my faery gentleman surface. The king was just on the other side of me, and he started swimming toward his rival. "I don't know who you are, but —" He pulled back a fist.

Quickly, I tore off my mask and shoved it at the other faery. "Please," I said. "It is you I want! Don't hurt him, your majesty!"

The king's eyes widened, and then he laughed. "Do you know what you've done? Do you know what your fate is now?"

"Wh—what?"

"This mask is made from the leaves of my bond tree. And its binding magic will deliver you there. It doesn't matter who fucks you, in the end. You will be trapped here forever. You will not be able to take her to your own lands, sir. One way or another, I will drink in your power, but it would have been so much easier if you had let me be the one to claim you. So much more pleasant for both of us. Now you will both be trapped here."

"My power? I don't have power."

"Your fertility, your lust...they put off power that will now belong to me. Everyone who comes to my revels gives their power to me. Go on. Wait for him."

Indeed, I was starting to feel an irresistible pull to that forest path now, and it was scaring me. I had made a terrible mistake, and there was no help for it. I should have listened to Alexandra. I shot one last look at my faery man. *I'm so sorry.* Then I started swimming for shore.

I reached the bank. My dress was soaked to my skin. For the first time, my face was bare without my mask, and the faeries stared at me. Somehow I felt more shame at them seeing my face than in the fact that I had been wearing a semi-sheer dress all this time.

The female musician, in particular, looked at me like she knew I had lost a battle with temptation. Some of the other girls, girls without masks, looked at me with pity.

Oh god, what have I done?

Of all the paths that led away from the revels, this path was the deepest and darkest. The trees hung over it, so tall and thick, that they blotted out the stars and moon almost entirely. The forest was full of ancient, hulking rocks and thick brush. Once I had hurried out of sight of the revels, I could barely see one foot in front of me.

I saw lights ahead. Shivering, I approached the three handmaidens, the same ones who had dressed me for the revels. Now they had serious expressions on their faces. They stood in a small clearing, each holding a torch. They placed the torches into mounts atop posts, giving a soft light to the immediate area. All the light seemed to be swallowed up behind them, by a tree with a thick trunk and very smooth white bark, with vines trailing from its branches. This, I thought, must be his bond tree. It held enchantment, different from all the other trees in the forest.

"My dear little human," said the one who always gave me my mask. "Now you are a part of the revels forever."

"Is there no way out of this?"

They glanced at each other. "You were told the rules."

"But—I didn't know the consequences."

"Weren't you? You knew that you would belong to the king if you gave away your mask. Don't you know that the rules of the faery world will lure you and trick you if you do not remain strong? I'm sorry. Our job now is simply to prepare you."

My heart was sinking at my own foolishness, and yet even now, I wondered what my choices were. I was a prisoner at home just as I would be here.

They drew closer to me. One of them untied the hook fasteners at the back of my neck so the fabric covering my breasts fell down, while the other lifted the petals of my skirts. I tried to fight them, tried to hold the skirt on. One of them swatted my hand.

"You know it is no use to fight," the dark haired one said. "Please don't make us subdue you!"

I let them drag the dress off of me. I was naked except for the gold at my throat, my wrists and my ankles, and the slippers. My breasts looked very round, my nipples hard, betraying the tiny quiver excitement still worming around deep inside of me, despite my terror.

I tugged at my hair so it covered my breasts. Now the cool of the forest touched every inch of me. My skin looked so pale and exposed.

"The gold, we will leave," said the fair one. "The king likes it."

"I thought the king isn't going to have me," I said.

"No, but that is all we know. What does your mysterious man like? We don't know him."

"It wasn't supposed to go this way," the redhead added. "But perhaps your heart knows after all. Perhaps you will still find happiness here. Come..." She took my hand, and the dark haired one took my other. The fair one walked just behind me. They urged me to step toward the tree. Some of the vines dropped down lower, like long green snakes. I remembered the faery woman with her hands caught above her head by the vines. But these vines were more numerous.

My fear sharpened. "What is going to happen?" I cried, trying to turn around to run. They immediately anticipated my move and gripped my wrists tight. The fair one shoved me forward. My slippers stumbled in the grass.

One of the vines whipped out and grabbed my wrist. The faery women let go. Now when I tried to bolt, the vines snagged me. I whirled around, so I was facing the handmaidens now, and the vines caught my other wrist. They pulled me back, sliding up to my elbows, so I hung from the branches of the tree like a struggling insect in a spider's web. I kicked my legs. "Please, put me down!"

More vines slithered up from the ground and caught my kicking feet. They spread my legs a little so that I felt the lips of my pussy draw apart. I wrestled and it was no use. "Please!" I cried again, more feebly. I hung in the air, splayed out in the shape of a star.

The faery women watched with those impassive expressions. I think they felt sorry for me but there was nothing they could do.

I stopped struggling, but I was breathing hard. At least, I thought, I had not given my mask to the king! My faery man would be gentle with me; I knew he would.

The vines shifted their positions to support me a little better as I hung there, and one of the faery women took out a blunt golden blade which glowed with enchantment. Her hand moved toward the short dark hairs between my legs and I tried to cringe back. More vines moved around my hips to force me into my position.

"It won't hurt," she said. "This is the king's request, but I expect your singer will like it too."

She started to slide the golden blade along my delicate skin, shaving me completely. It didn't hurt at all; in fact, the blade was soothingly warm and almost tickled as she moved it around every careful contour. Worse, as the golden blade and the woman's careful fingers shifted my folds, working all the way down, the other two hand-maidens removed my slippers.

"No—please!" I started struggling again. They had told me those slippers were my tie to my own world, and I felt the loss of them as they slipped away from my feet. My bare toes felt as exposed as anything.

Worst of all, just then, the king walked into the clearing. The handmaidens bowed to him and presented him with my slippers.

He walked up to me, holding one in each hand. I was so ashamed that my first instinct was to look anywhere but at him, but I told myself to be brave. I lifted my chin. But my trembling betrayed my fear.

"Princess Evaline," he said. "This is what I hoped to see. You, in the loving embrace of my bond tree. It won't let you go until you've sated it for the night. But I think you are very much ready to be sated." His hand moved toward my naked cleft, and I battled against the vines with a cry of dismay, but he drew back again and shook his head. "I still cannot touch you. I don't have your mask. It is a pity, but I will still enjoy your power. You aren't the first girl to be caught by another man at the revels. Why don't you sit down and make yourself comfortable?"

The vines drew me back against the trunk of the tree, and I was able to bring my legs closer together again. My toes found small footholds. The bark was completely smooth; soft, even. It was contoured somewhat, as if ready to accommodate my body. It was a relief to have something to lean on and stand on, and not to just hang in the air. I tried to shift one of my feet, from tiptoes to heels, but there was a small smooth knob poking out of the tree just behind my bottom. I shifted my hips, trying to get around it, and it jabbed me in the tailbone. Then the vines, looping around my shoulders, pulled me back up to my tiptoes again. But as soon as they had hauled me up, they loosened. They didn't really support me.

I started sweating, realizing what was happening, what

the king wanted from me. The small knob was meant for me to sit directly upon. The only way to avoid it was to keep standing on the very tips of my toes.

"Come on, Evaline," he said. "At least give me something. I invited you here. I saved you from your stifling home, didn't I?"

I shook my head.

"Didn't I do you a favor?" he insisted. He glanced between my legs. "You protest, of course. Demure little creature. But even now you are dripping wet. Do you feel how wet you are?"

I whimpered, but I couldn't deny that my body and my mind had different opinions of the situation. My mind didn't even want to think of home, of how shameful all of this was, and how I would never fit in back home again—if I ever saw home again, which I likely wouldn't, although that was hard to truly comprehend. In the core of me, however, there was a building heat, and a part of me almost wished the king was able to touch me right now.

"Where is he?" I cried. "Where is my faery gentleman?"

The king glanced back. "I don't know. He should be here by now. I certainly hope he hasn't abandoned you or I suppose you might be here for a while."

Chapter Fifteen

WILL

I watched Evaline struggle to shore, but I kept one eye on the king. He glanced at me with his mouth twisted in a somewhat unreadable expression. It was hard to tell if he was angry or pleased. He seemed a bit of both.

"Whoever you are, you will be trapped here too," he said. "As long as you keep her mask for your own, you will be drawn to her again...and again...and again. Still, you're lucky. If she had not given you her mask, I would have disposed of you."

"You bastard," I said. "You stole my voice, too."

"You should have known better than to tangle with the faery realms," he said. And then he gave me a small, mocking bow. "I will see that the princess is made ready for you."

He forged his way to shore, and I followed just behind him. He hurried through the dancers, toward the dark forest path. One of the faery maidens I had danced with before gave me a playful shove when she saw me holding the mask. "So you've gone and done it, have you?"

"I don't have time," I said.

The faeries were dancing around me now. I shoved past them and they let me go, cheering me on to claim her. I must get to the princess.

But as I was setting foot on the path, the female musician poked her head out of the shrubs. "Psst!"

I walked closer to her, and she pulled me down into a crouch beside her.

"I should not be talking to you," she whispered. "But... I have never seen a lure enjoy my music the way this girl did, and—the yearning for my days of freedom is almost unbearable now."

"A 'lure'?" I asked.

"One of the girls the king targets for the revels."

"Are you also one of his girls, then?" I was alarmed. Her music was beautiful but now I saw the pain in her face.

"Not in the same way. We musicians have made bargains with him, for one reason or another. Once the revels were a truly glorious celebration, but now there is a shadow upon it, thanks to the king. He targets people who are especially vulnerable to the illusion of freedom he provides, and tries to convince them to join him forever. But like all faeries, he is still bound by rules. He often fails. Evaline's sisters were able to resist him, but I know she failed because she loves the music so much, and it breaks my heart to think our music has ruined her life, that it convinced her to stay in this trap forever."

"It wasn't you," I said. "It was me. Is there any way to break the enchantment?"

"You would have to—" She paused and shut her eyes.

"You would have to kill him. And—it won't be easy. He is quite strong; I doubt any human could take him in a duel."

Kill him. That wasn't what I wanted to hear when I had vowed never to take a man's life again, but...what were my options? I could not let Evaline and myself be trapped in this endless dance. "I'm not so bad myself," I said.

She gave me a small smile. "You are a bit arrogant, sir, but...you might be the one who can manage it."

"How can I best kill him?" I asked. "There must be a way."

"If you can get him to let his guard down and kill him in one strike before he realizes what is happening...but of course, he is very suspicious of you. I don't know. I'm sorry...I suppose it was no use for me to try."

I looked at the mask in my hand. "I'm not sure about that. I know what gets a man to let his guard down..."

If I fail, Evaline...please forgive me.

Chapter Sixteen

EVALINE

My feet were trembling. I could not sustain this position. I was starting to grow terrified that my toes would slip and I would *fall* onto the little knob.

"Relax, Princess," the king said. "You should get used to this now. The tree needs to make its own connection with you in order to draw your power. Be good or I think you will find that it has grown by the next time."

"Please," I whispered, but I knew my pleas were no use. My legs were quivering. Slowly and gently, I eased my back entrance against the knob. It felt somewhat slick like it had been prepared for me with oils. I lowered my heels in the smallest intervals, and the knob pushed into me. I moaned.

I had to look away from the king. I couldn't bear to see him watching me. I knew the knob was not very big and couldn't really hurt me, but I never felt anything push into me there before. I was frightened, sweating, desperate to get it over with, feeling its smooth round hardness stretching me inside.

I gasped. My ass clenched around the knob of wood, but my maidenhood was still empty, displayed to the open air, and more than ever I wished someone would touch me there.

At least, now, my heels were on the ground, and I was no longer in such a precarious position.

My faery gentleman finally arrived. I strained against my bonds with relief. I wasn't sure if the relief was because I thought he would save me, or simply that he would touch me and hold me.

His eyes shot to me and widened slightly. In the dark, it almost looked like he blushed. He would be tender with me, at least I knew that. But I didn't know if he could stand against the king.

His expression hardened as he looked away from me again.

"Well, here you are," the king said. "I was just informing the princess of what a predicament she has tangled herself in. And whoever you are, now you will be a part of my revels too."

"You have it all wrong," the other faery said. "I never wanted her mask in the first place. I just wanted to teach her father a lesson and claim a reward. I'm no faery." He swept off his cloak, and a strange quivering shimmer passed over his body, changing his appearance.

My faery man, who would not give me his name until I gave him my mask, was not a faery at all, but Will the cobbler, the man I had allowed to be whipped, even though I knew he had followed me into the faery realm.

I sunk into a dread so deep it was like drowning.

"You are a human, after all," the king said. "I

wondered... But it was a good glamour, I'll give you that. It's always the accent that gives one away."

"Hmph, well, not much I can do about that." Will shot me a snarling look of disgust. "This *girl*," he said. "Her father wanted to know where she'd been going. He said that anyone who solved the mystery would have her hand in marriage and the kingdom to rule someday. I followed her here and brought back enchanted leaves from the grove, but her father claimed that I could have had them made myself. And then she—*she* flatly denied it all."

"I'm sorry." My voice was a whisper. "But—I truly wanted to believe it was you, sir. I know you have no reason to believe me, but...that's why I asked you to sing."

"Yes." Will practically spat the word. "She asked me to sing. That's all she cares about. But my voice was gone. And where did it go? I think I know where."

"You've caught me," the king said. "I stole your voice. But you see, we can't have one man stealing the show. These are my revels."

"I don't want your damn revels. I just wanted what I was promised. So, there I was, unable to sing or do anything to prove myself. I achieved exactly what the king asked for, and what did I get for my troubles, I ask you?" Will unbuttoned his shirt, revealing the bandages covering his back. Some blood had spotted through the white. Even without uncovering the wrappings, it was easy to see he had been whipped. "The entire court watched my punishment. Now, do you think I want this girl? Maybe to fuck her once, teach her a lesson. But not forever. I want a girl who is brave enough to stand up for something."

His words pierced my heart like shattered glass. Tears had already been threatening to stream from my eyes. I willed them back, but a few still broke through. "I made a terrible mistake," I said. "I know I did, and there is nothing I can say. But I wasn't the one who set up that contest; I didn't want to marry some unknown man just because he followed me to the faery realm. I wanted *you*, Will, but I didn't know it. I wanted you not because you were a faery, but because of your song, and our talks, and..." *Oh, the things you did to me!*

He had been so tender then...

"Anyway, I can't blame you if you don't want to marry a jaded soldier with a bad leg and calloused hands." His voice had changed a little, grown softer. I could tell, then, that a part of him still wanted me. I couldn't blame him for being angry with me after what he'd endured but it gave me hope.

But then he looked at the king. "Give me back my voice and give me her slippers to prove I was here, and I'll give you her mask."

"Please—Will, please!" I cried. "I do want you— I want you to be my king! I want to rule with you the way we talked about—together!"

The king looked like he had unexpectedly stumbled on a treasure. "Done," he said, without hesitation. He handed over the slippers, and then gave Will a rough kiss on the lips, and Will made a face. He touched his throat and sang a tentative note. This time, it came out as clear as a bell. Just hearing one note of his wonderful voice tore at me. I wanted to hear that voice forever.

The king was staring at my mask in his hand, his fingers practically twitching with eagerness. "See, I've kept up my end. Now, give it here."

I was helpless. Every attempt to so much as move my limbs, and the vines tightened around me. The small penetration of the knob reminded me who I belonged to, that my body was not my own any longer. And now it would be forever.

"This is not *fair*," I said, angrily. "I gave *you* my mask, Will. I was told that no one could take it from me. But now, you give it to a man I don't even love?"

Will thrust the mask at the king. The king clutched it between both hands, and then he turned to me, his eyes shining like a wolf emerging from a forested wood.

"Now—now I can touch you. Finally—you are mine. All your beautiful sisters have tempted me, all these years. I had hopes for every one of them, and they all turned out *boring*." He mashed his hands to my breasts, taking them both in his large palms, staking his claim on me. I stiffened. It was done now, and I was not sure whether to give in because I had no choice, or to will myself not to feel it or respond to it, because he was not the man I had loved, but that didn't matter anymore. The man I thought I was falling for had given me up.

Chapter Seventeen

WILL

This is it. My one chance.

The faery king had turned his back to me. I was of no importance to him now, just a human who had surrendered his claim. His full attention was on Evaline.

For a moment, I could see the man I had killed on the battlefield. I could feel the pressure of driving my sword through him. I saw blood, I heard his cries.

But then I saw the king's hands roughly grab Evaline's breasts, and all I could see was the pain in her eyes.

I took out Jeannie's knife and plunged it into the king's back. Just like when I was in the middle of the fight, I didn't hesitate. Hesitation was too dangerous, and in the end my fighting instinct conquered all else. I knew the spot that would bring a swift end, but still I gave it a twist, because he was a faery and I didn't trust his magic.

"She's afraid of you," I growled. "Get your hands *off* of her."

I needn't have worried. His blood began to flow from the wound immediately, as he made a terrible, choked sound. He stepped back from Evaline, clutching his chest. One more step back, and he stumbled. I had to catch him or he would have knocked me down with him as he fell. I gripped his shoulders and lowered his body to the dewy grass.

"You...human...," he managed. "It's all yours now."

The light died in his eyes, and I pulled the knife out.

Evaline looked at me with shock. "You—you killed him."

I straightened up. "It was the only way to save your life."

"You *did* save my life," she said. "Will, I meant it when I said—"

"Shh. I know." I stepped up to her and gave her a kiss. Her mouth opened hungrily to mine, and I could practically taste her relief, that I had not betrayed her after all. "My princess," I said.

"You weren't really angry at me?"

"I was angry at the time, at your castle; of course I damned well was, being tied up there and whipped like a criminal. But I also saw you, looking so small and pale and lost, with your parents' will bearing down on you. It's no wonder you didn't defend me. Even if I had been able to sing, I don't think your father would have let you marry me."

"He'll have to, now. He will have to give me that much." She looked firm. "But—" She tugged at the tough vines holding her fast. "The tree won't let me go!"

"I'll get it," I said. I wiped the knife off on the grass and then moved to cut through one of the vines.

As the blade bit the vine, a little sharp quiver of pain lanced down my own arm. "Ow—!"

"Did you cut yourself?"

"No, I—"

I realized the distant music had stopped, and that footsteps were approaching. The musicians and dancers were coming down the path toward us, led by the woman who warned me about the king. I hastily grabbed my cloak and draped it over Evaline, which conveniently enough, didn't just cover her up, but made her invisible.

I had a very bad feeling as the revelers all bowed before me.

"Hail to the new king of the revelers!" the female musician declared. She clutched her hands together.

"*What?*" I shouted. I grabbed her arm and pulled her hands apart. "What do you mean, new king of the revelers? Stop smiling! You didn't tell me that was part of the bargain!"

"I'm sorry, but we've been under the thumb of that man for so long! We wanted a new king—a king who would enjoy the music and restore the revels to their original purpose, not simply lust for more power."

"I can't stay here," I said. "I only came down here in the first place so I could marry the princess."

"You already have her mask," one of the dancers said. "Of course you can marry her. You're practically married already by our reckoning."

"I mean, back in Torina. *Her* kingdom."

"But why do you want to live in her kingdom? All of her sisters were lured here because they never got a chance to dance. If you go back there you'll just have to live under their rules."

I clutched my head. "So we could make it a better

place, damnit. To make up for everyone who died in those wars; to give my sister a good life! I'm taking Evaline home."

"Well, you can't," the woman said. "You're one of us now, and that is now your bond tree."

I said a few expletives that I usually reserved for solitude.

"Will," Evaline said. "Maybe we should listen and find out what the original purpose of the revels was in the first place. What do they want us to do?"

"Did you make her *invisible*?" said the mischievous little blonde faery girl I had danced with before.

"Yes. She is in no state for your eyes right now," I told her. "Fine, then. Tell me. What is the purpose of the revels?"

"Long, long ago," the musician said, "revels were always held in this pocket of the faery realm. People would pass through the Three Precious Groves, as they were known, and cross the river, to indulge in their need for music, dancing, and sex, in the fine night air. The revels were always governed by a faery who was the king of the revels. He would direct the proceedings and make sure the revels were the grandest party in all the land—decadent enough that they felt a little dangerous, but also that all the participants were willing.

"The kings of revels past particularly liked to open gateways to the human world in places where human girls were especially straitlaced. It's always girls, isn't it? I suppose that no matter where you go in the human realms, the women were not permitted to do as many things as men, are they? We never have human men here!"

"That is probably true," I agreed.

She continued, "He loved to see how human girls, who

had been told that they should never enjoy themselves, and were as shy as mice, would begin to let down their guard and dance and sing and laugh. He always felt that, after they went home, they probably felt more free forever after.

"Then, there was an incident when our king—this king—had been newly crowned. The duties as a king include keeping watch over the participants and making sure the guards are vigilant so that no one gets hurt. A man raped several girls, and a shadow fell upon the revels. The king took the blame entirely upon himself—he had not been paying enough attention. He made a pact with the oldest tree in the forest that from that day on, girls would be given a mask to wear, that was connected with the tree. And that no faery could touch them unless the girl offered him her mask as a clear mark of her permission." She paused, as if the memories were beginning to upset her too much, before she took up the story again.

"The king found that by forming a connection between the enchanted trees and the consummation of two people, he could tap into the energy of their love making. It fed him sexual power like a drug. He never intended this consequence to begin with, but soon, he began to obsess over ways to make the connection stronger, to increase the surges of power. And thus, now the tree has been enchanted so it will hold your princess until you make love to her."

"How can I end this enchantment for good?"

"It is actually quite simple." One of the handmaidens who I had watched dress Evaline came forward now. "Stop making the masks and the connection of power will begin to fade before long. The revels will be as they once were. We should go back to protecting girls the old-fashioned way—by looking out for each other and quickly expelling anyone who doesn't follow the rules."

"And now?" I looked back at the vines holding my invisible princess, and I hoped I already had a guess as to the answer.

"It's too late for her now," the mischievous faery girl said. "The tree will release her when she's ready..."

"All right," I said, trying to look like I wasn't so eager to get to it. "Well, we still have to figure out what we're going to do about this, but for now, the lot of you, get out of here."

I turned to her, stepping close enough to touch her, but at first I did not. She looked up at me, her eyes shining with trepidation and yearning.

She had never looked so beautiful, like ripe fruit waiting to be picked. Her dark hair spilled across her shoulders, with the glinting strands of gold laced through it, the gold choker at her neck above her pale collarbones. I hardly knew what to admire: her breasts, round and full; her prone limbs wound with green vines and bands of golden bells. Every inch of her was exquisite. Her skin shone faintly with sweat. Her pussy had been shorn bare, and reminded me of her mouth—two bare lips and her little pink bud poking out like the tip of a tongue—warm wet hunger inside.

I put my hand on the tree trunk behind her, and as my fingers met the smooth white bark, I could feel her desire like it was a living thing—like honey on my tongue and shimmering music in my ears. I realized that she was mounted to the tree, connected to it. No wonder her expression was a little pained.

"My god, Evaline," I breathed.

She was breathing hard, her ribcage rising and falling. How had I ever resisted her the first time?

And yet, this was the first time she had seen me as myself. I didn't touch her right away. I wanted her to see me too, to know if this was what she really wanted.

"Will," she whispered. "That is your name. I'm glad you are just yourself now. It suits you."

"But now," I said, "it seems I am also the King of the Revels. It wasn't what I planned."

"We'll just have to see, won't we." She moistened her lips. "I hope you aren't in too much pain."

My back burned, but pain was a funny thing. It melted away if your mind was somewhere else. "No," I said.

"Your eyes are different," she said.

"My eyes?"

"They're golden."

Like his. I was disturbed at the thought. But it was hard to think about anything but the sight of her, and my sense of her need.

"Please touch me, Will. I've been waiting for this moment."

I didn't have to be told twice.

Chapter Eighteen

Evaline

His hand slipped between my legs and I immediately let out an absolute wail of relief.

"My good little princess," he said, pushing my hair off my neck as he stroked me there. "You're not so quiet anymore."

His hand trailed down my neck, and then he dropped a line of kisses from my shoulder to my ear, even as his other hand continued to tease and stroke my folds. Then he put his mouth to mine, his tongue dipping into me, and his fingers clamped down on my clit and slowly twisted it a little. I moaned into his mouth and gently bit his lips. Our kisses were voracious.

He slid both hands up along my thighs and hips, his thumbs tracing the tender place where my legs met my body. Sometimes his touch was almost ticklish, and I writhed in my bonds. Every place he touched felt twice as sensitive because I was so helpless; I could do nothing to stop him from touching me wherever he liked. His flat hands slid up the plane of my stomach, as his hips drew closer to my hips. I felt his erect sheath resting against my stomach, just beneath the fabric of his trousers.

My kisses grew softer when his hands moved to my breasts; my attention was distracted now by the pinching at my nipples. Every nerve in my body seemed to be connection with every other nerve, sending jolts of sensation between my breasts and my core. My ass had grown shockingly used to the knob and now it almost seemed too small. I needed something to fill me, to sate me.

Instead, just the taste of his mouth and his hands on my breasts, and I started to climax, my pussy pulsing and clenching at nothing. I whimpered. It was a swift little fluttering sensation that only made me need more.

My arms strained. I wanted to grab him. "Will, fuck me," I cried. The old Evaline was entirely unraveled. "Please, I can't stand it."

He took a step back and regarded me. "I just don't want to forget this moment," he said. "We'll never have another first time."

It was like being forced to say a long round of prayers when a feast was put before me, and my stomach was ravenous. He looked delicious, even with those unfortunate bandages around his chest. I wanted to touch him everywhere; the stubborn set of his stubbled jaw, the strong arms that I yearned to have around me, the slightly troubled line of his brow. The eyes that could be commanding or tender, changing as fast as passing clouds.

He unlaced his boots and stepped out of them, and unbuttoned his trousers. His cock was erect and magnificent—but even before, when I took the head in my mouth, I had noticed how large and thick it was. I hoped I could take its entire length.

He let his trousers fall to the ground, and I saw now that his leg was marred with scar tissue around his knee and puckered gashes up his thigh.

"I wanted you to see all of me as I am," he said.

"Will, what happened?"

"I was knocked to the ground during one of the battles and trampled by a horse—and a few boots as well, I think. It's all a blur. I would certainly have lost my leg, or maybe died, if my regiment hadn't had a very skilled healer. All told, it's healed up very well. I'm pretty steady on my feet. But it's stiff. I'll never be a graceful dancer anymore. Not unless I wore the enchanted cloak, but...besides the fact that I would look like someone else, I have a feeling it won't work anymore."

"Does it hurt?"

"Sometimes, just a bit."

He had lost friends in my father's wars, and sacrificed something of himself too, and now he worried I would be disappointed that he couldn't dance?

"My dearest Will," I said. "I think it might be a blessing that we will rule the revels, and not Torina. We wouldn't have been able to take over until my father died, and that might be thirty years away. Thirty years of pushing back against the strictures of court? We might lose our minds. But here, we will be able to make a life of happiness from the very first day. And we will restore the revels to their original purpose, giving people a place they can safely be free. I would like to be queen of such a place. I know just what girls like me need."

He lifted one eyebrow and smiled. My words had satis-fied him, I could tell. He didn't reply; I think maybe he was a little embarrassed to show such vulnerability to me. He stepped in to wrap his arms around me. "What you need, eh?" he said. "I hope you're ready for me. Because with all that out of the way, I'm going to claim you. First slow, and then hard, and then we'll see."

I could only nod.

His hand moved down between my legs again, and he spread my slit wide open with his fingers, and then stroked my clit again for a moment, until I was arching my neck back and low sounds of desire drew out of my throat.

I felt the tip of him fit inside my entrance, and I tensed with fear. I didn't know how much it would hurt. But his hands slowly slid down my back, like he was smoothing the tension out of me, and as he did so, he started to enter me. I could tell he was moving as carefully as he could not to cause me undue pain, but the girth of him was still a shock. And unlike the small knob that had already penetrated me, he was a living thing, his cock pulsing a little as it pushed inside me. Its small motions were not entirely predictable.

I let out a ragged little scream as he broke my maidenhood.

"Shh, darling." He smoothed my hair. "It feels so good and tight inside you."

The length of him kept coming, pushing through me, finding deeper and deeper places to go, and he kept caressing me and kissing me, until finally he gave a small thrust and I shuddered against him. My arms were starting to fall asleep, but somehow the vines seemed to sense this, or maybe the tree simply approved of the fact that he was inside of me. Their grip on me slackened enough that I could lower them almost to my sides.

"I feel so full," I moaned. "I can't—it's too much."

"Is it really?" His voice was like a purr against my ear, and he gently nibbled at my earlobe. "I feel your pleasure," he said. "I can see how the king got addicted to this connection. But I'm sure I will have no interest in continuing this magic with anyone else, as long as I can take you this way."

I let out a shuddering sigh at the idea that he might be able to claim me like this again and again.

He kissed me deeply as he stroked against me on the inside, and my body began to adjust to him. I realized how much I was burning. No part of my body felt like my own. I was pinned between Will and the tree, and now that he was the King of the Revels, the tree was like a piece of him as well. Every bit of me was being bound and penetrated. His tongue fucked my mouth as his cock fucked me on the inside, and I didn't want to do anything but fall into the sensations of it and sob with pleasure.

"Yes, my princess. Just relax. I've got you." His arms held me so close. I relished the feel of his tender embrace, his chest against mine, the sweet, vulnerable feeling of our naked skin pressed together. The smell of him was like the forest itself. He increased his speed now; he didn't want to wait. His cock was pounding into me and the steady pressure of it was stirring something inside me. Every stroke scratched at the surface of some well of exquisite sensation.

"My king," I said.

"King," he grunted. "Don't know if I'll ever get used to it."

"Will you sing for me every night?" I asked.

"Anything your little heart desires."

"Oh, Will—Will!" My pussy was starting to tighten and clench around him, and the sensation was mounting. I was so wet inside that even his thick cock was gliding up and down inside me easily. And then I was coming again, with a rush of heat that trickled down my thigh. The aftershocks were still hitting me as the vines abruptly released their hold of me. My weight collapsed into him, and my arms were completely weak from straining and struggling against the vines for so long. He held me, and dropped a line of kisses on my face from my jaw to my earlobe.

"Oh, but you're not free yet," Will said.

Chapter Nineteen

WILL

The princess, it seemed, could climax if you just touched her right. Meanwhile, I seemed to be caught in a state of slow, torturously mounting arousal.

But I had noticed the trees weren't the only object of interest. The rocks around here came in some convenient shapes.

"Put your arms around my neck and your legs around my back," I said.

She obeyed. She was so small that I could carry her easily. I put one arm around her, keeping her pinned to my cock. Then I picked up the cloak and draped it over a boulder that was about as tall as my waist, to provide a layer of softness. I sat her bottom on the edge of the rock and reluctantly withdrew from her.

"Lay on your stomach," I told her. "With your legs over the side."

Her eyes widened a little, but she did as I said, settling

onto her stomach, wrapping her arms around the boulder to hold her position, and letting her legs drape down over the side for me. Her feet were still a ways off from touching the ground. Her pussy was still glistening and pink, swollen with desire. I picked up her legs and stepped close to her, fitting my cock between her lips, slowly sliding along her wet slit, but not penetrating her.

She was a little stiff now.

I leaned over her, letting my stomach gently rest against her round, firm ass. "I told you I was going to fuck you slow and then fuck you hard, didn't I?"

"Mmhm..."

"And now that I'm in the faery realm, I'd better tell the truth." I could no longer stand the anticipation of my own release, in any case. I thrust my cock into her hard, and was rewarded with a full-throated cry, "Will, oh god, Will!" I was never going to get tired of her crying out my name.

Now she was positioned so that it was easy to bear my full strength onto her small body. Her back arched. My cock thrust into her mercilessly, and I could hardly keep my mouth shut either. "Evaline..." It felt so damn good; she was so slick but so tight, and I could feel her inner walls trying to draw me in deeper again. My princess was never really satisfied.

Her small body was rocked, her cries growing almost anguished, but she didn't ask me to stop. I drove into her with all the tension I had held back; I had shoved so much down inside me when I came back from the war. I could put it into her now, and she could take it, and make it disappear, at least for this moment.

I had a vision of her, the way she had been back home, with her hair pulled back severely, all her skin covered, her stiff dress, her pale sweaty face so miserable. Contrasting that with the girl before me now, naked and spread, taking my cock again and again, and that was enough to drive me over the edge. I clutched her soft curves as I pumped my seed into her. I had never had such a lengthy orgasm; the pulses just kept coming.

I had never felt anything so good and right in my life. I was groaning her name now as my climax was still slowly winding to an end.

"That was fucking worth the wait," I gasped.

I leaned my body over her now, and wrapped my arms around her, gathering her beneath me. I kissed the nape of her neck. She made a little contented cooing sound now, like a dove.

"I don't know what happens now," I said. "But I know it will be better than what has come before, because I have you."

"I know it will," she said, with feeling. "I get to dance and sing. Maybe I'll even learn to play an instrument. But...I wonder where we live. Where we sleep. *Do* we sleep?"

"We must," I said. "Because I'm pretty tired."

"I think I could sleep for a whole day straight," she agreed.

I finally slid out of her, and helped her to her feet. She was shaky like a baby animal, and laughed nervously. "I guess I'm not used to so much exercise."

I didn't see her dress anywhere.

"The handmaidens took it away," she said.

I handed her my shirt. "It's long enough to cover you up. I don't see any blood on it."

"I don't care if it does, anyway."

I put on my trousers and boots, and I tied her slippers onto her feet. We returned to the revels, which were still in full swing and merrier than ever. As we walked into the clearing, the faeries cheered and started singing bawdy songs. A few high elves sniffed and removed themselves to the drink tables. Evaline looked slightly horrified, blushing deeply.

"I think we'd better indulge them and listen to a song or two," I muttered.

Someone pressed goblets of wine into our hands. The dance increased its pace, but we didn't dance, but rather were shown to chairs at the banquet table. The faeries started to bring out fresh dishes of food to us; heaping piles of fruit and cakes and sliced venison and some things I could not even identify, but my nose was definitely approving of the smells wafting my way. Despite myself, I realized I was ravenous. I had never sat down for such a feast in all my life.

"Who is in charge here?" I asked one of the faeries bearing a tray of honeycomb.

She laughed. "You are, your majesty."

I clutched my head. "I mean—don't I have to be crowned?"

"No. You're not that kind of king."

"I need to go home to my sister."

"And I need to tell my parents what has happened!" Evaline said.

"Your parents? Who wants to see them again?" the faery asked, as if she knew Evaline's parents.

"But I do! I must!" Evaline grew immediately distressed. She had been through so much; I didn't want to see her cry. I clutched her hand under the table. "We *must* make one final trip home," I insisted. "We have families. I'm damn sure not going to be your king if you won't let me tie up loose ends at home."

"The king is not supposed to leave the revels. But...I'll see what I can do." She put down the honeycomb and left us there. Eva shot me an anguished look, and I rubbed her shoulder. "It'll be all right," I said.

"I hope so..."

It must be admitted that it was a strange world I had found myself in, and one I didn't entirely like. I didn't feel like I was in charge of anything. If I was the king, I deserved to know the rules. After a moment, I threw down my napkin and told Eva, "Wait here."

I walked over the musicians and waved my hands at them. "Stop the music!"

The song wound to a halt. I put my good leg on the platform and held out my hand toward the drummer. He took it and I heaved myself up and lifted my hand until I had everyone's attention.

"Listen," I said. "Apparently I am your king now, like it or not. And I'm not opposed to the idea, but I'm not going to put up with being a prisoner. I want to finish dinner, and then I want to see where my bed is—I hope I've got one—and have a good night's sleep. Then the princess and I need to go home—however that can happen, it must happen. And after that, I want a briefing as to how this place works, how it can be improved, and how I can bring the revels to places where we are needed."

The faeries all looked rather stunned.

"A briefing?" one of the men said. "What is a 'briefing'?"

"Do I have any advisors?" I asked.

"We are all happy to advise," said a faery girl with little antennae on her head like an insect. "What do you need?"

"We flow with the music," the drummer said. "We don't have a lot of rules."

"I can't be a king in a realm of anarchy," I said. "We must have a little bit of order. It sounds like that's how the last king got into trouble." I huffed at the nervous faces surrounding me.

"We've never had a human king of the revels before," a goblin girl murmured.

Evaline giggled. "Will, I think this is going to be a learning experience for all of us," she said. "But the good thing is that there are no soldiers and no wars here."

Indeed, I started to feel as if the revels were almost like the afterlife. But we weren't dead. No, we weren't dead at all. Maybe they were more like a strange pocket of joy in a harsh world, in some ways not unlike the traveling circus I had once attended as a boy. When we finished our meal, the handmaidens showed to a little house made of wood tucked in the forest. It was built around one of the trees. Although it was small, it was as beautifully decorated as a music box, and as comfortable as could be imagined. A fire was already crackling in the hearth, and a bed piled with down-stuffed quilts was waiting nearby.

"Milady, do you need help undressing?" the fair hand-maiden asked.

Evaline glanced down at my shirt and stifled a smile. "I think I can manage unbuttoning a shirt."

The handmaiden nodded and left us alone. The door shut behind her, leaving us alone again.

I started to unfasten her buttons, sliding her shirt away from her breasts. I had seen them glowing pale in the moonlight. Now I saw them golden by the fire. She was still wearing all the golden ornaments, but the contrast of my white shirt, worn soft by many washings, falling from her shoulders... She was so beautiful, I could not help but cup the fullness of her breasts in my hands and play with her temptingly hard nipples.

She sighed, and put her hands to my hips, sliding her fingers just past my waistband. She unbuttoned my trousers and took out my cock, like it belonged to her now, stroking it to full attention again.

"Should we, again, so soon?" she asked.

"I said I would fuck you slow, and fuck you hard, and then we will see... I believe we've come to the 'we'll see' part of the evening. Are you sore?"

"I am," she admitted. "You weren't kidding about the 'hard' part." But she glanced at me with a willing gleam in her eyes. "Could we just have a night like the first one, Will? When I took you in my mouth, and you..."

"Come here." I picked her up, and she laughed. I was very grateful that she didn't question that I could carry her, despite my slight limp. I dropped her on the bed and climbed over her the other way, touching my cock to her lips. She took me in her mouth, and I spread her legs open a little more so I could get to her pussy.

"I like you shaved here," I said. "Like a water nymph."

She paused, freeing her mouth to speak. "And what do you know about water nymphs?"

"Naughty etchings."

"I'll accept it."

I dragged my tongue down her sweet, smooth skin, to her clit, and then to her entrance, and she groaned happily.

"Get back to work," I said.

"Yes, my king," she said, and I thought how I would never get tired of hearing *that*. Her lips and tongue slid along my length, and by the time the night was over, we had not slept as much as we intended.

Chapter Twenty

❧

EVALINE

I didn't know that the sun ever rose in the land of the revels, but I suppose it did for me now because I was a part of this place. We slept right through it, but as the sky outside our window turned crimson with sunset, I thought we had better get up. I had to face Mother and Father.

We followed the path I knew well by now, through the Three Precious Groves. And at the end of it all, my hand-maidens dressed me in my old shift, corset, and nightgown. My clothes had never felt so tight and heavy, and this was only my nighttime wear. If I was going to face my parents, I would have to dress properly. Will, lucky man, at least had comfortable clothing.

The faeries said we could return to our home until midnight.

What then?

The revels would find us, wherever we were, as long as there was no barrier forbidding faery magic.

There were ways to bar faery magic.

I was more than a little afraid that Mother and Father would no longer treat me as their precious, sheltered daughter. That maybe we would be trapped in the human world forever, after all.

But we both agreed that we must go. We couldn't leave our families to wonder what had become of us.

We stepped out into my bedroom, and now the time between the faery world and ours seemed to match. It was dusk outside. A guard was standing in the room, apparently watching for my return, and as soon as he saw me, he blew a horn. "The princess!" he shouted. "The princess is here!"

Oh, dear. This was not a good sign. "Please," I said. "Don't make a fuss." But it was too late. More guards entered and they seized Will the second he came up the stairs.

"Let him go!" I snapped. "Where is my father?"

Father huffed into the room a moment later, followed by Mother. They looked at me with such terrible expressions that I felt a little light-headed. I was a different girl in *their* world. Perfect, obedient, silent.

"Where have you *been?*" Mother cried. "Oh, Eva!" She looked at my nightgown and then around at the guards. "Get out, get out. The princess is not fit to be seen. Take the cobbler out too."

Will struggled, and looked at my father. "You can ask him—" He jabbed his head toward the guard. "I emerged from the other realm accompanying the princess. You can't deny that I discovered the secret and fulfilled your bargain."

"We'll see," Father said.

"No!" I shouted. "No, 'we'll see'! Will is my rightful husband now."

Father and Mother both looked at me, and Mother said, "Shh. Calm down."

"I will not calm down. Let him *go*. He tells the truth and doesn't deserve to be treated this way."

Father hesitated, but then he nodded at the guards.

"Let's get Evaline properly dressed and then we will discuss it," Mother said.

I relaxed just a little as the guards released Will. Father waved them all out and shut the door on us. Mother didn't say a word as she opened my wardrobe.

"Take off your nightgown," she whispered.

I had never realized before how afraid I was of my mother. It was strange, for a woman so quiet and gentle. She had never beaten me. She never yelled. It was her disappointment, her endless judgment. That was all it took to make me cower, because I had never known anything else. I had always wanted to please her, and yet I could never suppress my desires for the very things she told me I could not have.

I pulled off the nightgown, and she took one of my plain gray dresses out of the wardrobe. Each dress was almost like the others, although that one was one of my least favorites, because the neckline was so stiff and high that it touched my cheeks.

She walked behind me and tightened my corset strings. They tended to get a little loose at night, but she was more aggressive than the maids just now. I knew she wasn't doing it out of vanity to give me a slender waist; of course she didn't give a damn about that. I could feel her anger in every tug.

"Stop, I can't breathe!" I snapped.

"It will be good for you, then," she said. "You must bear a little discipline after what you have done. You are not marrying that peasant. You're going to the convent."

"I'm not."

"You must. I see that now, it is your only hope."

"I want to talk to Father."

Our words sounded as strained as my laces. She helped me into my dress, and I stood there stiffly, letting her do all the hooks and buttons. But when she tried to touch my loose hair, I stepped back.

"No," I said. "I will wear the shawl but I won't put my hair back."

She looked at me, and our eyes battled in silent contest. Mother was not one to enjoy verbal fighting. She used her eyes to win fights, her big sad eyes. I always backed down, but this time I held my ground.

I had never held my ground before, and she looked a little flustered.

"Come then," she said. "You're right. We'll talk about this with your father. He must make a judgment."

I followed her down the long stone hall, the hems of our heavy skirts dragging along the ground.

In the throne room, Father was waiting, and so was Will. His eyes rested on me, and he looked a bit grim. But there was a little humor in his eyes too, strangely enough. Maybe it was what they called "gallows humor". It had been such a strange day, that there was something a little funny about us meeting again now, with me looking so demure, when just hours before I had been bound naked to a tree.

I wondered if he had been able to talk to his sister yet. Probably not. The throne room was empty of courtiers, just guards, but he still kept looking around like he was hoping to see someone.

"Let me get this story straight," Father said. "Evaline, you have been going to another realm at night, a realm with leaves made of precious metals and gems, and this man followed you there last night."

"Yes," I said. "Just as you asked him to do. His story was true the very first night, and yet you whipped him."

"You denied it yourself."

"I did, but...that was because I didn't want to be forbidden from going back."

"It is a faery realm?" Father asked.

"Yes..."

"You realize that you have done wrong?"

"No." Now my inner stubbornness was trying to rise up, although I had to battle against those disappointed gazes bearing down on me from the thrones.

"I don't think we have much choice," Mother said, speaking now mostly to Father. "We can't hand our kingdom to some common man."

"Then why did you open the test to everyone?" I cried.

"She has to go to the convent," Mother said. "Look at her. She is not my good sweet Evaline. The faeries have done something to her."

Father nodded grimly. "Sir, I will reward you for solving the mystery, and you can go home," he told Will.

I knew I had to say something. I had to tell them the truth, I supposed. *You don't have to worry about rewarding Will or sending me to a convent. We're going to the faery realm and never coming back.*

But this was where my stubbornness began to falter. I was so afraid to tell them. *Maybe I shouldn't have come back at all!* But then they would never know what became of me. Should I have let them wonder? No, Will wanted to return as much as I did, to speak to his sister.

My stomach was in knots over it all.

They were my parents; they should be my responsibility, but Will looked at me, as if saying, *Do you want me to try and handle it?* Any minute he was going to open his mouth, either way.

"You have grown very disobedient," Mother said. "Well, we all have to answer to God."

"Yes—yes." I bit out the words. "But Father is the one who dragged our country into a war, and sent men off to die."

"What does that have to do with anything?" Father asked.

"Will lost loved ones in that war. It had nothing to do with him and he gained nothing from it but a bit of soldier's pay and a lifelong injury. And in the end, you gained nothing either. That battle was a stalemate and you just hosted the Dorvanians to a dance! How does that make people feel? How does that fit with our religious ideals? In the realm where I've been, there is no war. That place exists to give people a place to escape and be free. All my life, you have told me what is right and what is wrong, but somehow all the things that are wrong are the very things that make me happy! And the things that are right only bring people pain. I would suffer for the good of my people, but I am tired of suffering for no reason at all!"

They looked at me with stunned expressions. I don't think I had ever strung so many words together in their presence in my entire life, much less said them with such force.

"I'm going to marry Will," I said. "And I'm going back

with him to his realm. Will is not a mere peasant at all. He is already a king. The King of the Revels."

"Eva!" Mother got to her feet. She looked lost. "If you think for one moment that we will let you return to that place— We must do what's best for you." She looked at Father. "But what can we do? The magic...it *hunts* her, doesn't it?"

"We will shackle her in iron and send her to the convent."

This was precisely what I had feared. I was not sure the faery magic of the revels would reach me.

"And as for him..." Father looked at Will.

"Your majesty," Will said. "You know that all I have done is to be your loyal and obedient subject. When I was called to serve in your army, I laid down my tools and took up your sword and shield. When you called for men to find the answer to your daughter's disappearance, I risked my life to follow her. In the faery realm, the King of the Revels was about to claim your daughter as his own, and I drove a knife into his back. That was when they named me the king in his stead. Now, I have a duty to return there. You don't need to offer me any reward. Just let me go."

He had certainly phrased that story well.

But was he leaving without me?

No, that could not be. I knew he was a clever man, my Will—he had already tricked the faery king.

"Very well," Father said. "But you had better never bring the revels to my kingdom again."

"Don't worry about that. You have no more daughters," Will said.

They let him go, but not before he gave me a brief, reassuring look.

One of the guards brought two heavy iron shackles.

When he moved to locked them around my ankles, I screamed. The iron burned me, my flesh marked red where it had touched.

"What has happened to her?" Mother cried.

"The faery magic has bound me," I said. "I didn't know, but...it makes sense. I—I made a sort of pact, while I was there. Please, you must see that I belong there now, not here."

"Oh, no, dear, this is...this is beyond the pale," Mother said. "Can we put cloth around the shackles so they won't burn her?"

The guards brought scraps of thick cloth, and tied them around my ankles, then tried the shackles again. This worked, and I knew this meant Will could not touch the shackles either. No one would see them under my dress, but my steps were heavier than ever.

Chapter Twenty-One

Evaline

The guards watched my every move. I tried to be patient. Luckily, since it was already evening, my parents soon retired to their bed and I went to bed as well. I knew Will would come for me as soon as he could.

But he didn't, and it was a torturous night. I could feel the call to the revels; I missed the music, and lust boiled within me.

In the morning, I searched for his sister.

"She was here," said the nurse in the infirmary, "but she left last night with her brother."

"Where did they go?"

"I don't know, dear."

I started to feel apprehensive. I knew Will would not fail me on purpose, but perhaps there was nothing he could do.

I sent a message to Will's house in town, just in case,

but before I could even hope to receive a reply, Mother said I was going to the convent this very day.

"Any delay is a risk," she said. She tried to touch my cheeks, and I pulled away.

"Someday you will realize it's for your own good," she said, beginning to weep.

"Someday, maybe you will realize that you have ruined our relationship and done nothing for the good," I said grimly.

"Eva...all I have ever wanted to do was shield you from harm."

I knew my mother truly believed this. She had grown up the same way. But we had reached an impasse.

A part of me thought my life was now over. Another part of me held out hope. The revels could travel. The revels would find me. Will would find me; he would feel the call to find me the same way I yearned for him, every moment.

I sat in the back of a carriage, which traveled for eight hours, rattling my bones over roads that were a mixture of rough stone paving and dirt. The convent was perched up a rocky hillside path. It was lonely here. The grass and trees were a deep summer green, and warm wind blew on my face. I think I might have liked it, in some ways...if circumstances were different.

The sisters gave me an austere, gentle welcome. I think they were used to naughty nobles being packed off to their convent, because the young woman named Sara who gave me the tour kept comparing everything to royal life: "We don't have any balls here, of course, but we do have quite a good time with the cheese making", and "I'm sure you're used to a very grand church with an organ, but there is something nice about our small chapel, I've found."

"Are you a princess too?" I finally asked her.

"I was of the noble class," she said, in a rather vague tone that made me think I should not ask questions about her life before.

I had a tiny room, but it was all my own, and a black dress that was actually less confining than the ones I was used to. The convent was very quiet, and the sisters were sweet and welcoming, but of course I was missing Will and the dances dreadfully. Was he there without me? What if I never saw him again? What if I was never touched like that again?

At night, I had a terrible time sleeping. I was always looking for a clock that wasn't there. I was always peering under my bed, or listening for something. The iron shackles were still locked around my ankles, and I had to be careful when I moved, not to touch them, or my skin would burn with sharp pain that took days to fade.

Days passed. Much of our time was spent in the chapel. I was always quick to volunteer my hands for work, because the only thing that kept me from going mad was keeping my hands busy. I learned to make bread, and helped pick the summer harvest. I helped spread tomatoes in the sun to dry. I was allowed to write letters to my sisters, but I hardly knew what to say. No one ever saw a tear in my eye, no one ever heard my sobs, but I poured them into my pillow at night.

And then I started getting sick in the mornings, and worry flooded through me every day that it went on. Weeks had passed, and Will had not come. Now it seemed that something was wrong with me. I might die here, and Will would never know...

After heaving into my chamber pot, I went to sneak it out to dump in the outdoor privy (we all had to take care of ourselves here, no servants to be found), and opened the door to find Sara standing there.

"You might as well tell Sister Maria before it gets worse," she said.

"What?"

"You're pregnant, aren't you?"

"Pregnant?"

"Weren't you heaving with morning sickness?"

"Is that why?" I whispered.

"I'd expect so, if you've had any dalliances before you came here."

My mouth gaped open before I said, "I'm having a *baby*? I thought I was dying!" I stumbled back into my room and sat down. And then I did cry. I didn't know if I was happy or sad. I was carrying a piece of Will inside me, but I might never see him again. And... "Will they take my baby away?" I asked.

"They'll probably find it a family," she said. "I'm sorry, Eva. I know what it's like."

"Please don't tell anyone," I pleaded to her. "I'm...I need to think about it first."

At night, I made plans to escape. Maybe I could find someone who could remove my shackles...but who? We were miles from anything.

At the convent, we always gave food to beggars, and shelter to women on the run—often women who had been beaten. One full moon night, an old woman came to the door, clad in a ragged cloak. The sisters welcomed her in the door and immediately offered her a bowl of soup. She shared our meal with us, eating and drinking in silence, and I know everyone was wondering why she had taken the long lonely walk up the hill at her age.

"What do you need?" Sister Maria asked her.

"You don't make this place easy to reach for an old woman, do you?" she croaked. "Just a bed for the night and I'll be on my way." She glanced at me. I glanced back. I had not mistaken it—she wanted to talk to me, I could tell.

Oh please, I prayed. *Let her be a messenger from Will.*

That night, instead of turning in, I crept to the hall where we put up guests for the night. The old woman was waiting for me there, where the moonlight poured in the tall windows.

She held up a key.

A beam of hope spread through me, as if the moonlight had brought me an angel. "Did Will send you?"

"Will," she muttered, in a tone that was not quite what I hoped. "I daresay he took credit for my spell. I gave him an enchanted cloak so he could get to the faery realm. I gave him that cloak because he sang for my son Michael and gave him a peaceful death, because he had an honorable heart. Because I wanted him to be the king of Torina. Torina!" she repeated, shaking the key. "Not the Wicked *Revels*!"

"It was somewhat of an accident," I said. "And besides, my father is still in good health...and his father lived to be eighty. He might rule for another twenty years, and if Will tried to argue with his policies, it would only make Father mad and he would cling even tighter to his original plans... It would be a mess."

"Yes, well, I've considered that," the old woman said. "And so has Will. He did send me, and he has been trying desperately to save you, but the iron you wear bars him from reaching you. He has been searching for help, and I said I would help. But I still want what I asked him for. I still want an heir for Torina, and revenge for my son's death. And so, I will unlock your shackles. You will go home tonight. But I ask one thing."

I was getting rather nervous now. "What...is it?"

"I want the son you bear."

"My child? I— Surely you must know; if you lost your own son. I can't give you that. *Anything* but that!"

She waved her hand. "Shh, shh, not now, dear. Not now. I want you to raise him to be a good and fair king. And then, when he has grown, I want you to give him back to the human world, so he can claim the throne of Torina when your father is gone."

When he has grown... That was a long way away. A time when children leave their parents, one way or another.

I put my hand to my stomach, although I was only six or seven weeks along. "Yes," I said. "I will give Torina a king."

Chapter Twenty-Two

⁂

EVALINE

That night, my ankles were free. That night, the passage opened for me. I traipsed down the stairs, so light I barely felt the grass beneath my toes—for I immediately took off my slippers this time.

My first handmaiden was waiting for me, and she beamed upon seeing me. "Princess! You've finally come home."

"Yes." I shoved my nightgown off. "How is the king?"

She laughed. "You've changed a lot since the first day I met you. The king is...well, he's fine, but he will be happy beyond words to see you. I have a new gown for you, befitting a queen." She dressed me in a gown made with layers of blue-gray fabric as thin and ethereal as cobwebs. Just like my last dress, it was just slightly sheer, but it had sleeves—loose and bell-shaped. It still plunged low in the front and back, and it fastened at the back of my neck as the last one did, but also wrapped around my waist with another fastener there. Will would have no trouble sliding it off of me if he so wished. It fell a little longer and softer than my first dress, however, and felt more regal. It had a belt made of leaves, much like the mask, which clasped around my slender waist.

The second handmaiden gave me the same golden jewelry as I had worn before, which still matched beautifully with my new dress.

The third handmaiden no longer gave me a mask. She took out the little blunt golden blade. "The king's request," she said. I throbbed with renewed excitement as she lifted my skirt and shaved my nether lips naked again. Then she sent me to the river.

The boat was waiting for me, and Will was standing in it.

I ran to him, and he stepped forward and held out a hand to help me inside. He clutched me against him and the boat swayed. We both stumbled and almost lost our balance. "Let's not do that again!" I cried. Then we laughed.

"Evaline. I'm so sorry. I moved heaven and earth to find you, I sent messengers and spies to check on you, but those damned bits of iron..."

"Messengers and spies? Why didn't you tell me?"

"I didn't want to get your hopes up, only to fail. At least I could see that you were safe enough, in a convent."

"You should have told me," I said. "Even if I never saw you again, at least I would have known."

"That's what my sister said. I fought her about it. I figured you already knew I would do anything to find you..."

I looked at him. He seemed different. He looked the same, I suppose, except for his golden eyes. Still more human than faery on the surface, but he seemed taller than I remembered, somehow. Stronger. He was finely clad now, in a doublet of brown velvet and had golden buttons on his boots.

"You look like a king now," I said. "You carry yourself like a king."

He smirked in a pleased way. "Jeannie said I've gotten even more obnoxious than before, ordering everyone around. But half of it is because I was so crazed to find you."

"Your sister? Is she here, then?"

He nodded. "I can't wait for you to meet her, and tell you everything I've been up to. But first, darling...I hope you're as hungry for me as I am for you."

I smiled. "Maybe more. I've been in a convent."

"Well, *I've* been watching everyone else have fun." He pulled me onto his lap and lifted the oars, putting them in my hands. "Why don't you take a turn here?"

"I have to row? What will you—" I cut off as his hand pulled up my skirt and his fingers shoved between my legs.

"Go on," he said, pumping his fingers against my clit. "It's a lazy river, I don't think it will give you any trouble. I see your handmaiden followed my directions. You're nice and smooth and already so wet for me."

I dragged the oars through the water, but I was not rowing very fast. I spread my legs a little wider as he pushed two fingers into my entrance.

"I'm going to lead you through the revels. And then I'm going to pin you to that tree," he said. "I want to see every fleeting expression on your face. I want to take your clothes off, slowly, and tease you as I do, with my tongue, my teeth, my hands, and finally I will take you with my cock—" His fingers thrust deep into me, a preview of what was to come, and the oars flailed in my hands— "until I must carry you to your bed, and then I have a surprise for you."

"Oh, you do, do you? I bet it's not as good as the surprise I have for you." The words leapt out of my mouth before I reconsidered that the surprise also had a slightly unpleasant caveat. The witch's bargain.

He looked like he wanted to ask about my surprise right away. Then he suddenly wrapped his other hand around my waist and held me tight, stroking my hip, with a touch that conveyed a world of yearning. "Eva, I've missed you," he said. "They say the revels has showed human girls how to be free, but it's saved me too, unlocked me from my bitterness. It's pained me to see the other dancers, without you there. I haven't sung a note. I'm waiting for you."

"I'm here now," I said softly, stroking his cheek.

Chapter Twenty-Three

WILL

I quickly came to realize that being the King of the Wicked Revels was basically being the host of the wildest party in all the known realms. Which was no small task, when you think about it, although I'm not sure the former king had. If the revels was an escape from all the troubles of the world, I had to make sure it was a good one. I talked to the musicians, the chefs, the winemakers, the seamstresses. I made it my business to know their names and their jobs, how they used magic—which they did use, in intimidating abundance. Most of all I needed to make sure the dance was safe but without losing the edge of danger that made it an exciting escape, a place where it was possible to let go of one's inhibitions. I think some of them were annoyed to have their new king poking around and meddling, but it helped keep my mind off of worrying over Evaline.

Well, to a certain extent.

I never really stopped thinking of Evaline.

But now she was here, and I would never let her go.

I had been disbanding all the magic of the masks and the trees that had so entranced the former king. I think he was a different sort of man, to woo all of Evaline's sisters, and who knew how many other women over the years. I was more of a one-woman sort of fellow.

But I wanted that one woman very badly. There was one spell I would never disband. I liked that when Evaline was bound to the tree, I was completely in control of her, and completely in tune with her, so that I knew exactly what would bring her the greatest satisfaction.

That night, I gave Evaline everything I had promised her, and she gave me everything I could dream of. My once-nervous little princess was now a wanton beggar for my touch, aching to be bound and mounted to my tree and fucked again and again.

Finally, I took her down and carried her across the threshold, and now that I had finally satisfied my burning hunger for her body, I could hopefully begin to satisfy all the buried dreams of her soul.

"Will...," she said, struggling in my arms. "Put me down. Did you get all of these for me?"

I had filled the room with instruments. A harp, a lute, a mandolin, a violin, flutes, pipes, drums; even an concertina, which no one here knew what to do with, but there it was.

"I know you dream of making music yourself," I said. "Well, the trouble is always deciding what to play. I wanted you to have every choice to mess around with. If you settle on something, we can always give the extras away, but maybe you'll be brilliant at all of them. Or maybe you won't be brilliant, but you'll simply enjoy it."

"It's perfect!" she said, running her fingers over the different strings. "You're exactly right. I've never even gotten to touch instruments before. I hope the musicians will show me what to do."

"I think they'll be thrilled." I gave her another moment to tap the skin of the drums, to blow on the flute, and then I couldn't stand it anymore. "What's my surprise?"

"Oh, *your* surprise? Well..." She took my hand and placed it on her stomach.

I met her eyes. "This doesn't mean...what I think it means, does it?"

"It's a son, Will. At least, that's...that's what the old woman said. It's a baby, at least. But that's the only thing... the old woman..." Her eyes cast down.

I hardly heard that at first. "A *son?*" I picked her up again. I wished I was more agile to swing her around.

"Yes. But...when he comes of age, we have to send him to Torina. That was the bargain I had to make. The old woman said she gave you the cloak that allowed you to do all of this in the first place, in the hope of putting a good king on the throne. Our son needs to be that king."

"I see," I said. I scratched my chin, considering all of this more deeply. "It's hard to imagine even raising a child in a place like this, now that I think of it."

"He will certainly have a different kind of life," Evaline agreed. "Even if we shield him from some of it. But...that might be exactly what Torina needs. Anyway, it's a long way off. I thought it was fair. I didn't have much choice, but...daughters usually go away to marry. For us, it will just be...a son going away."

"It is true that I wouldn't be here without the old woman's aid," I said. "So I think it was the right decision. We'll have a long time to make sure he's ready."

Epilogue

EVALINE

Eighteen years later...

"Have you packed everything? All your clothes?" I knew he had, but it made me feel better to fuss.

"*Yes.* I packed ten hats, one see-through shirt and a pair of leather pants. That's enough, right?" Roland smirked.

"Ha, ha," Will said. "You think this is going to be easy?"

"He gets that from you," I said. We were teasing each other, but really, I was on the brink of tears. How had eighteen years passed so quickly? How had my chubby cheeked little baby turned into this man who was eager to *escape* the revels? He thought they were dull and oppressive. He was excited to go to the human world, no matter how much I warned him about it.

So it goes, I told myself. I had more sympathy with my own parents with each passing year. I would never agree with a lot of their choices, but I also understood how easy it was to second guess oneself when it came to children. I wasn't always sure what to do with Roland, growing up among the wild faeries, and it was even worse when the girls came along. The faery women had to keep reminding me not to coddle the girls more than the boy.

Jeanette and Alexia, at least, were easier than Roland. He was a "fire sign", the elves and goblins said—they were big believers in astrology. The girls had followed in our musical footsteps, Netta as a violinist and Alex as a composer, both of them collaborating in a sisterly harmony that made me miss my own sisters. But we all made music together, many a night. I favored the flute because I could carry it with me everywhere I went, and Will still had the best singing voice in the family.

"I wonder who you'll meet there," Jeanette said. "You're going to shock the pants off those human girls."

"They don't wear pants," I said. "Not ever."

"I *know* that. It's an expression."

Will looked at his pocket watch. "You'd probably better get along the path. Your grandparents are waiting."

"Try and be...patient with them," I told Roland. They had accepted him as the heir. I suspected some magical persuasion was involved, but who knows? Maybe they just missed me. I'd exchanged letters over the years, trying to smooth the way for his arrival. But I still imagined Roland would be the talk of the town for a long time. Maybe not *always* in a good way.

"Yes, you'd damn well better behave yourself," Will said. "Or I'll come out there."

Jeannie was cleaning up the dishes from our farewell dinner. She had married a wood elf man shortly after her arrival. Happy as she and Olvar seemed, she still spent a lot of time at our house fussing over the kids, since she never had children of her own. She paused and lifted her eyebrows. "Oh, to spy on the scenes to come," she said.

"I don't think the best play in the world will top the arrival of Prince Roland to fair Torina," Olvar agreed. "Perhaps we could try a scrying pool and ask for a glimpse."

"You'd better *not*," Roland said. "Anyway, my parents have given me a pretty big reputation to live up to."

"Good luck, Rol." Will clasped his hand and then pulled him in for an embrace. "Write every day."

"Every day? Sure...good luck waiting on a letter every day. But I'll try for every week." Then he hugged me.

I was getting a little teared up. Actually, a lot. Jeannie quietly handed me a handkerchief.

Netta and Alex didn't fare much better. We were all a mess as we fumbled out further goodbyes and waved to him as he set off on the path.

"Don't cry!" Will said, although I thought I saw a tear in the corner of his eye as well. "This is a good day. A new day, for our old home, and the fulfillment of a promise. I know he's going to be a wonderful king, and I think he's going to find a wonderful queen out there as well, once the season begins."

"And I'm not there to see it...!" I cried. But it was a good sign that Torina had a 'season' these days. When my sisters were growing up, my mother didn't allow such festivities.

Later that night, I was still feeling very sentimental as I came to bed. Will sat beside me, wrapped his arms around me, and kissed the crown of my head. "Still as gorgeous as the day I met you," he said.

"I'm feeling quite ancient, seeing Roland off. It really feels like yesterday..."

"Well, you were still a young thing yourself when he was born. And how far we've come. But he's ready for responsibilities of his own, and I meant what I said. I do think he'll be a good king."

"I hope he's *happy*," I said. "I understand my parents better now, yes, but sometimes I still think of how gloomy that castle was for me, and I shudder. There is nothing I'd rather be than your queen."

"And there is nothing I'd rather be than your king." He slid a hand beneath my dress, encircling my breast. "I, for one, will be glad when all the children have found their own happiness, at this point. I love them more than anything, and yet..."

"They *are* distracting. And always hungry." I smiled.

"I could use a distraction myself," Will said. "The girls are out with their friends. I would like to remind my queen where she belongs." One of his hands freed the clasps of my dress while the other hand slid lower.

"That," I said, "is impossible. I know exactly where I belong."

Thank you for reading! I hope it was a pleasant escape! If you enjoyed this book, consider leaving a review. Amazon will ask you to give a star review when you're done, but that doesn't actually count. I don't know what that is. Amazon is trickier than a fairy. And to make sure you don't miss a release, sign up for my mailing list, and come chat with me on Facebook. Is there a fairy tale you'd like to see? Let me know! I like less common ones too and I already have a few in mind, but next up...Rapunzel meets a prince of the shadow lands.

Fairy Tale Heat Series

Every book is standalone and can be read in any order, although some characters might pop up in later books!

About the Author

Lidiya Foxglove has always loved a good fairy tale, whether it's sweet or steamy, and she likes to throw in a little of both. Sometimes she thinks she ought to do something other than reading and writing, but that would require doing more laundry. So...never mind.

lidiyafoxglove@lidiyafoxglove.com

Made in the USA
Las Vegas, NV
30 January 2022

42655749R00094